WRAPPED UP WITH A RANGER

A SMALL TOWN MARRIAGE OF CONVENIENCE ROMANCE

KAIT NOLAN

TAKE THE LEAP PUBLISHING

WRAPPED UP WITH A RANGER

BAD BOY BAKERS BOOK 2

Can a grumpy former Ranger find lasting happiness in a marriage of convenience with a sunny single mom?

After losing his leg, former Army Ranger Holt Steele is building a new life and a new business with his friends. Sure, he never expected to put small-town baker on his resume, but he finds he likes the quiet, simple life. If only he didn't like the sunny single mom who works across the street--or her adorable kid--quite so much.

After escaping a controlling husband, event planner Cayla Black has one focus--growing her business and maintaining a safe, happy home for her daughter. She has no time or interest in a man. Not even one who charms her child with Disney songs and keeps turning up like a mind-reader to help without being asked.

But when her ex's conviction is overturned on a technicality, and he shows up to reclaim his wife and child, Holt intervenes with an outrageous lie. The only way to fix it is to make his falsehood the truth. As they struggle to convince everyone that their marriage of protection is real, these two reluctant hearts fall deeper, until the lines between the fiction and the dream begin to blur, and they have to risk it all to protect the family they didn't know they wanted.

1

Holt Steele eyed the absolutely packed parking lot of Elvira's Tavern. "Who decided karaoke night was the way to celebrate the acquisition of our business license?"

His business partner, Jonah Ferguson, drove on past. "Drinks we didn't pour ourselves were the designated celebration for the approval of our business license. It just so happens that the lone drinking establishment in Eden's Ridge is hosting karaoke night on the day it happened."

From the backseat, the third member of their trio, Brax Whitmore, snorted. "He's conveniently not mentioning it's an opportunity for the two of you to seek out some prospective female companionship, and that he's shamelessly willing to take advantage of those pipes of yours to impress the female population with your karaoke prowess."

"Hey, we can't all be as lucky as you," Jonah protested. "And anyway, you still owe me a drink or something for dragging your ass down here so you could reconnect with Mia in the first place."

"And again, I remind you that you didn't know she'd be here."

They were both right, but none of them were under any delusion that Brax would have reconciled with his wife if he *hadn't* come to Eden's Ridge and been forced to overcome a decade's worth of stubborn misconceptions when she'd turned out to be the contractor hired to renovate their building.

"Details. You still wouldn't have been here if not for me." Jonah slid the truck into a space a block away with the practiced ease of a country boy used to squeezing an extended cab pickup into the tight confines of a street that had been built when vehicles were considerably smaller.

"I suppose I can buy you a pity drink since I'm the only one of us currently having my bed regularly warmed by a beautiful woman."

"Hey, I could have options if I wanted them."

"And does the not wanting have something to do with a certain blonde who just headed back to Syracuse last week?" Holt asked.

Jonah scowled and slid out of the truck. "I told you, there's nothing going on with Rachel. We're just friends."

Holt hummed a noncommittal noise and glanced at Brax, who smirked. They both had eyes enough to see the tension simmering between their buddy and the woman who'd taught them all to bake as part of an experimental therapy program last year.

"Besides—" Jonah started back toward the tavern. "Since it's my hometown, I've gotta be discreet. Doesn't matter that I'm over thirty. Any of my shenanigans get back to my mama, I'm gonna hear about it. I don't look forward to that any more now than I did when I was sixteen and she somehow found out that Ashley Chapman relieved me of my virginity in the backseat of my car. No man should have to endure a safe sex talk with his mother more than once in a lifetime."

They all shuddered, though they shared a mutual adoration of Jonah's mom, Rebecca, who'd unofficially adopted Brax and Holt when they'd moved to town to go into business with her son.

"See there, Broadway, you're morally obligated to impress some tourist women with your voice to improve Jonah's odds. Especially if he gets enough beers in him to try singing himself," Brax added.

Holt had no intention of getting up and singing. He wasn't embarrassed and didn't have stage fright. He just didn't want the attention the whole thing would bring. Women liked men who could sing. While he might appreciate some companionship, he didn't relish the looks of pity or revulsion when they found out his military service had claimed part of his leg. He'd made peace with being an amputee and outstripped all of his doctors' expectations with how he'd taken to the different prostheses, particularly the carbon fiber running blade that was his favorite. But there were plenty who'd view him as less of a man for the loss, and he wasn't much up for screening the potentials.

Then again, with their bakery about to open, maybe he should get up there as a form of free advertising. If people were intrigued, it might get them to show up. Holt knew the food would keep them coming back once they tried it.

Flanked by his friends, he stepped inside the bar. For a few moments, they stood in the entryway, eyes adjusting to the low light, each of them scanning the building in the tactical evaluation that was second nature after their stints in various branches of the armed forces. He'd committed the layout of the place to memory months ago, so it was the crowd he assessed as someone on the little stage performed a rendition of "Bohemian Rhapsody" that was so bad Freddie Mercury himself was probably on his way to haunt the tone-deaf son of a bitch. Holt wished he was packing tranq darts just to save the audience from further ear hemorrhaging. He could argue it was a public service. Probably.

"I'm gonna need something a hell of a lot stiffer than beer to endure this," Jonah muttered.

"Won't we all." Holt led the way toward the bar, automatically searching the patrons for a familiar face he knew he shouldn't be looking for.

Behind the bar, Sariah Hitchens worked the taps with an economical grace. The bottom edge of a Marine Corps anchor tattoo peeked out from the sleeve of her fitted gray t-shirt, but it was the haunted eyes that gave her away as someone who'd served. Like recognized like. She'd come here for the equine therapy program a few months back and hadn't left. Holt couldn't fault her for it. The mountains of East Tennessee were a good place to heal and a good place to build a life.

"What'll it be, boys? It's Coronas usually, right?"

"Nope, we're here to celebrate," Jonah announced. "A round of that twenty-year Macallan that Denver keeps for special occasions."

Her sleek black brows arched. "What are we celebrating?"

"We're all official and shit. Bad Boy Bakers can legally open its doors. Got our business license today."

Sariah didn't even try to hide the smirk. "Bad Boy Bakers? That's really what y'all went with?"

Holt felt his cheeks heat and crossed his arms.

Jonah just shrugged. "I mean, we've gotta work with what we've got." He gave an exaggerated flex of his biceps, coaxing a laugh out of the serious bartender.

"Fair enough. Coming right up. And hell, I might grab one for myself just because Jed's finally finished committing crimes against Queen."

"Thank God." As Brax made some creative suggestions about what could be added to the hapless Jed's drink to ensure he didn't make it back into the singing rotation, Holt turned toward the stage to see who was coming next.

And there she was.

A familiar, curvy little blonde stepped up, trailed by a couple of women he didn't know. Cayla Black. Event planner. Their across the street business neighbor. And the woman he couldn't get out of his head, despite his best efforts. The intro began, and Holt recognized "I Won't Say I'm In Love" from *Hercules*. He wondered how many million times Cayla's daughter, Maddie, had made her watch the movie. Or maybe this had been one of Cayla's favorites when she'd been a kid. It had certainly been one of his sister Hadley's.

Cayla launched in, her smooth, clean voice a breath of fresh air after the musical butchery of Jed. Her friends sang backup, the three of them obviously having a hell of a good time. It seemed like this might be some kind of bachelorette thing, because they all wore t-shirts with bling proclaiming *I'm with the bride*. He tried not to notice how those rhinestones highlighted her breasts and utterly failed. The whole trip across the bar, he lectured himself—again—about how she was absolutely off limits and not for him. As a single mom, she deserved more than what he had to offer. So did her cute-as-a-button kid. But it didn't stop him from flipping through the song catalog for something that would adequately show off his skills. If he was gonna do the thing, he was gonna *do the thing*. He punched in his selection just as she hit the last couple of lines.

The crowd hooted and cheered. Cayla took a little bow as her friends waved and began trooping off the stage. Because he was next up, he waited at the edge, holding out a hand for the mic as she neared. Her step hitched, her cheeks pinking as she laid her hand in his. The spark snapped all the way up his arm, singeing his good intentions at the edges as he closed his fingers around hers and helped her down the step.

"Hey, Cayla."

Those big brown eyes darted up to his and away again. "Hi."

"Nice pipes."

The blush deepened. "Thanks."

Instead of releasing her hand, he held out his other one. "I think I'm next."

She looked down at the mic, as if she'd forgotten she had it. Her cheeks headed toward fire engine territory. "Oh, um. Sure."

Damn, she was cute.

Avoiding eye contact, she handed over the microphone and scurried back to her table with several other women in matching t-shirts.

Holding back a grin, he stepped onto the stage himself, surveying the crowd as the opening bars to "Your Song" from *Moulin Rouge* began to play. Plenty of curiosity out there, both about who he was, whether he could carry a tune in a bucket, and certainly a fair amount of *Hello, Soldier* from more than one of the women in the audience. But it was really one woman he was thinking about, and he brought his gaze back to hers as he prepared to sing.

HE'D BEEN HOLDING out a hand for the microphone, not to help her off the stage. Cayla fought the urge to bury her flaming face in her arms as she dropped back into her seat. Would she *ever* stop embarrassing herself around the man? Seriously, it was a sign.

Zara Singh leaned over, her dark eyes lively with interest. "Girl, what was *that?*"

"Nothing."

Misty Pennebaker, the bride they were out celebrating tonight, picked up her drink, one of the local wines her fiancé Denver, who owned Elvira's, kept in stock for her. "That definitely didn't look like nothing."

Cayla waved them all off because Holt began to sing. The entire bar went silent as his voice rang out, clear and confident and performing one of her favorites. Not that there was any way he could know that. And as he hit the end of the first stanza, she'd have sworn he was looking at... her. Which was ridiculous. Foolish. And wouldn't matter, anyway. She wasn't looking for anything. Her plate was already overflowing with keeping her business afloat and her daughter safe and happy. There was no room for a man. Not even one who sang like an angel and made her want to lick those Army-honed muscles like a popsicle. Holt was just a nice guy. One who held a fondness for her daughter. She could enjoy his performance from a purely objective standpoint because he was one of the few present with any actual talent. It had nothing to do with the fact that it felt like he was singing to her. He wasn't *trying* to melt her panties. It was just an unfortunate byproduct of all that potent alpha warrior hotness.

Then, on the last line, he winked. At her.

Cayla's entire train of thought derailed as she tried to figure out what it meant. She was woman enough to admit she was hella attracted to this man. And on her confident days, she was pretty sure he was attracted right back. But over the past few months, as their paths had continued to cross, she'd gotten the impression he didn't intend to do anything about it. Maybe that was because of Maddie. Most men wouldn't want to take on a five-year-old. Not even if they seemed charmed by her. And that was entirely fine. It had taken far too long to rid herself of the last man who'd swept her off her feet to risk being swept again. Fool her once.

But Holt had winked. Hadn't he?

Unable to hold back the question as he left the stage to thunderous applause and whoops, she polled her friends.

"Oh, hell yes," Astrid announced, nodding hard enough that her cloud of gorgeous natural curls bounced. "I may bat for the other team, but I've still got eyes in my head. He totally winked at you."

Misty and Zara confirmed.

Celeste Keeling, the fifth member of their bridal party, leaned back in her chair, glancing across the room in speculation. "Pretty sure that was as open a declaration as there could be."

The certainty in her statement sent Cayla into an instant retreat. "We're just friends. Sort of."

"I would really love to have a friend look at me like that," Zara sighed.

"How exactly are you 'sort of' friends?" Misty wanted to know.

"Well, he's one of the guys opening Bad Boy Bakers across the street from my office." Okay, office was an exaggeration as yet, but once she finished spiffing it up, she'd be bringing clients there. It still counted as hers from the day she'd signed the lease.

"Go on," Celeste prompted.

Wanting to minimize the whole thing, Cayla shrugged. "I've been in and out over at the bakery a lot while they were renovating because of Mia. Holt ended up helping me out a couple of times with an emergency cake for some of the weddings I've done. It was just—I don't know—preemptive partnership. They'll be the only bakery in town, so of course they're going to end up doing cakes and other food for the events I put together."

"So he's one of *them*," Zara noted, grinning in the guys' direction. "I've been hearing all kinds of rumors, but I hadn't laid eyes on any of them myself."

Celeste fanned her face, as if there were a hint of a blush to mar the warm bronze perfection of her skin. "I'm pretty sure they'll be getting plenty of traffic on their looks alone."

Which had totally been the point when Cayla had thrown

out the name. But she'd been half-joking, in one of those awkward, embarrassing, couldn't-quite-keep-ahold-of-her-tongue-around-him moments. She hadn't really expected them to *take* the suggestion.

"Well, I say we can't just leave this as it is. We've got to encourage Fate a little bit." Before Cayla could protest, Zara hopped up from her seat and crossed the bar to where Holt sat with Brax and Jonah. While Lewis Washington, one of the co-owners of Forbidden Fruit Cidery, rocked out to "Don't Stop Believin'", she said something to Holt in her enthusiastic, animated way. Holt glanced in Cayla's direction and nodded.

Cayla desperately wished for the floor to open up and swallow her. That sinking sensation in the pit of her stomach got worse as Zara left the guys' table and went to the karaoke computer. What the hell was she up to? A smug, self-satisfied smile split Zara's face from ear to ear as she dropped back into her chair.

"What did you do?"

"Girl, I helped." She waved a hand toward the screen on the wall that listed the next song and performers.

Holt Steele and Cayla Black. "Don't Go Breaking My Heart".

As Lewis reached the end of his song and Holt rose from his seat, Cayla shot her friend a withering stare. "I hate you."

Zara just blew her a kiss. "You're welcome! Now go on up there and flirt!"

Cayla approached the stage as if it were a gallows walk. Holt already had one mic in his hand and snagged the other from Lewis as he stepped down.

"Nice job, man."

"Thanks! You're not so bad yourself."

Holt offered her the microphone, then continued to hold out his hand when she took it. Mortified all over again, Cayla thought about just stepping past him onto the stage. But that seemed rude and like a deliberate slight she didn't intend, so she laid her hand in his. The moment those long, callused fingers curled around hers, she steadied, and the noise of the crowd seemed to mute. Did he feel that electric hum, or was it all in her head? It had been so damned long since she'd felt legitimate attraction, and God knew, it hadn't been this... visceral with her ex-husband.

They took their places on stage, and he didn't release her hand, didn't look at the crowd. Nerves crashed down on her like a wave no longer held back, jittering in her belly, through her muscles. Cayla couldn't remember the last time a man had made her nervous in a good way. She was well aware she squeaked through her first couple of lines. When they hit the "ooo hoo"s, he gave a little yank on the hand he held, spinning her into him for a joint shimmy. The move so surprised her, she laughed, missing her next line. But it loosened her up. The taciturn former Ranger was *flirting*. In some dim, dark recess of her mind, she remembered how to do that. So she stopped focusing on the situation, on the audience, and focused on the man instead, looking into those piercing blue eyes that seemed to spark with humor as she fell into the call and answer of the song. By the time they finished, she was grinning.

At Holt's encouragement, she took her bow. He did the same, then escorted her off the stage.

"Buy you a drink?"

"Oh, well, I'm here for Misty's bachelorette party, and I've already hit my limit. I've gotta pick up Maddie from my mom's later."

"A soda then. Or lemonade? Singing always makes me thirsty."

"Okay, sure. Thanks." Cayla headed for the bar, aware of the warm press of his hand on her lower back as they navigated the crowd.

They placed their orders and waited as the gorgeous black woman behind the bar pulled them together.

"So how's everything going at your office?" he asked.

"It's going. There are still a million and one things to do around there before I can really see clients. The painting alone is taking forever. But kid, work, only so many hours in the day." She laughed, because she could move to a planet with a thirty-six-hour day and still never catch up. Such was life as a single mom.

"Sounds like you could use a hand. We're all available Sunday."

Cayla blinked at him. "Y'all have your own business to put together."

"It's mostly there. Got the business license today. That's why we're out tonight. Celebrating. Other than that, the renovation's done, all our equipment is in. We're just refining recipes and working out offerings and prices. We can afford to take a break to help you out. Besides—what's that saying? Many hands make light work. Does Sunday work for you?"

"Um." It seemed like there was probably a reason she should say no, but damned if she could remember why. "Yes?"

The bartender delivered their drinks.

"Good. It's settled, then. We'll see you on Sunday. Enjoy the rest of your party." He lifted his drink in a toast, curved one corner of that mouth that so rarely smiled, and headed back to his table.

Cayla scooped up her lemonade and made her way back to her friends, wondering what the hell had just happened.

2

"Remind me why we're here on our day off," Jonah wanted to know.

"Because she's a single mom who needs help, and we have time and capable hands." Holt wheeled his 4-Runner into the tiny gravel lot in front of the little house Cayla had rented for her office, parking beside her older-model Camry. Brax and Mia were already here. The flower beds had been weeded since last week. Not that it said much. The bushes out front were still scraggly and overgrown. They needed pruning at the least, yanking out at the best. He wondered what she had planned for the beds. Something bright and cheerful like she had at the little bungalow where she lived? Or something more sedate and professional? He hoped for the cheerful. Anything else didn't seem like it would suit her.

"And this has nothing to do with you wanting to bone her?"

Even knowing this was payback for poking at him about Rachel the other night, Holt shot Jonah an icy stare. "Watch your mouth, and no. I'm not looking for a package deal. I did my time raising Hadley." Not that he regretted the sacrifices he'd made for his baby sister.

"But you adore that kid."

It was true. "Maddie's my little buddy. That doesn't mean anything." *And if I keep telling myself that, maybe I'll believe it. Because both daughter and mother are way too damned appealing.*

He shouldn't have given in to temptation and sung with her. Well, it wasn't so much the singing as the dance he'd pulled her into because he'd wanted to wipe that anxious expression off her face. And to get a sense of the feel of those soft curves. The whole thing had gone against his personal code of being her friend and nothing more. But he just hadn't been able to help himself, and damn, it had been the most fun he'd had in longer than he cared to remember.

Jonah hit him with some not insignificant side eye. "Methinks the Ranger doth protest too much."

"Look, you were raised by a single mom. Wouldn't she have appreciated some help when you were coming up?"

"Fair point. And to be clear, I have no problem helping Cayla out with this. She's always been a sweetheart. I just wanted to bust your chops."

"I'll exact revenge in our next sparring match."

Jonah grinned. "Bring it, Broadway."

After a perfunctory knock, they went inside. Mia and Brax were already at work, applying painter's tape around the windows and all the trim. A neat stack of painting supplies sat in the middle of the scarred wood floors. There was no immediate sign of Cayla.

"Holt! Holt! Holt!" A little blonde dervish came racing toward him from the kitchenette.

He bent and scooped Maddie up before she could career into his bad leg. She settled against his waist, snuggling against him as if she'd been doing it for years. "Hey, Bumblebee. How are you today?"

"I'm good! Grandma made *pancakes* for breakfast this morning!"

"That is, indeed, an awesome way to start the day," he agreed.

Sobering, she reached up to press her little hand to his brow.

"Whatcha doing, kid?"

"Checking you for a fever."

"No fever. Why?"

"Mama says you're hot."

Mia snorted, and Brax choked on a laugh. Cayla, who'd been coming out of the tiny bedroom that served as an office, pressed both hands to her flaming cheeks and did an abrupt about-face.

"Out of the mouths of babes," Jonah intoned.

It took everything Holt had to repress the delighted smile. He shouldn't be delighted. It didn't matter that Cayla thought he was hot. He wasn't pursuing anything. He was here, with friends in tow, to help her out. That was all.

Lowering Maddie to the floor, he looked her in the eye. "Are you helping us paint today?"

"Little Miss Big Mouth will be watching movies on the iPad." Face still pink, Cayla emerged from the back, a stern gaze on her daughter.

Maddie's eyes were wide and innocent. "What?"

Cayla sighed. "Nothing, Munchkin. The iPad is in the office. Go pick what you want to watch, okay?"

"Okay, Mommy." She scampered down the hall.

As Cayla watched her go, Holt studied Cayla. Something about her seemed off somehow. Dimmer than usual.

"Everything okay?"

"Yeah, everything's fine."

She flashed him a smile, but it wasn't her usual sunny beam, and he recognized fake-it-til-you-make-it when he saw it. Something was definitely bothering her, and he didn't think it was embarrassment over what Maddie had blabbed. Was it something to do with the two of them getting their flirt on Thursday night? Was she upset by his admittedly mixed signals? Or was something else going on? As she looked around the room with something like yearning, it struck him that maybe he'd made a mistake, all but shoving their help down her throat.

Holt rubbed at the sudden heat in the back of his neck. "Listen, Cayla, I should have done this the other night before I dragged everybody else into this, but... are you okay with us being here?"

She blinked, focusing in on him with a faint frown. "Why wouldn't I be?"

"I mean, maybe you wanted to do everything yourself. To take ownership of the place. I didn't mean to minimize that. I just thought you'd get done quicker, and I basically told you we'd come instead of asking if you even wanted us to. Orders are kind of a hazard of my former occupation." And damn, the men of his unit would razz the hell out of him if they could see him now.

For the first time that morning, she really looked at him, those big doe eyes searching his face with cautious wonder. "It's really sweet that you even thought of that as a potential issue. And no, I'm thrilled y'all are here. I'm absolutely terrible about asking for help, but I'm sure as heck not going to be so precious as to turn it down when offered."

She stepped closer, laying a hand on his arm. The warmth of those slim fingers soaked into him, soothing some disquiet he'd carried for so long he barely even noticed it anymore except when it wasn't there. What would that gentle touch feel like on the rest of him?

"Anyway, everything we get done today will get me that much closer to being able to see clients here." This time, when she smiled, it reached her eyes. For now, anyway, she'd willed away whatever was bothering her. Holt was satisfied that whatever it was, it wasn't about him. He'd take that for the moment.

"And, hey, your business doing well is better for our business," Brax added.

"I consider this payback for all those pep rally and spirit week banners you painted back in high school," Jonah put in.

It was a startling reminder that they'd known each other for years. That this was her town, and she had a long history here.

Cayla laughed. "I'm surprised you even knew I'd made them, since I was just a lowly freshman to your senior."

"Easy to remember, since Lance Peterson had the biggest crush on you."

"He did not! He never asked me out."

"Yeah, that might have been because we gave him shit in the locker room when one of the guys found the epically bad poetry composed about your smile."

"Language," Holt growled.

Jonah winced, shooting a glance toward the sound of pattering footsteps from the back. "Sorry."

"What ever happened to Lance?" Cayla wondered.

"I think Mama said he moved to Louisville and became a banker or something."

"Didn't he marry Jenny Sheridan?"

As the two of them continued to swap small town gossip, Holt just shook his head. This whole thing was so alien. He hadn't grown up in a small town. Hadn't played high school sports. He'd been too busy busting his ass, working, making sure his baby sister was taken care of and that his mom didn't pass out and choke on her own vomit after her latest bender. His mom hadn't handled single parenthood well—or at all—preferring to fall into the bottle whenever her latest shit choice in partners disappeared, as they always had. She'd been nothing like Cayla. She'd never once put her kids first. Hell, maybe that was part of his fascination with Cayla. He had mad respect for everything she juggled on her own and the good, solid life she'd built for her kid. She was a truly good mother, on top of being sweet, funny, smart, and beautiful. And Maddie was—

"Holt! Holt! Holt!"

She came running in, the iPad in hand. "It's Maui! Do Maui!"

"Um." It was his turn to avoid everyone's gazes as Maddie held up the screen, paused at the key scene in *Moana*. He'd known singing for her a couple weeks back was going to come back to bite him in the ass. But he couldn't help it. After all these years, all the work he'd put into it for Hadley, he was programmed to sing along to all Disney tunes, and she'd been watching *Oliver and Company*.

"We're about to get to work, Bumblebee."

"Oh please, oh please, ohplease! Just one!"

"Yes, please, Broadway," Jonah smirked.

"Yeah, seriously. I've been hearing stories about this voice of yours," Mia urged.

Holt looked back at Maddie's pleading face and sighed. Damn it, she looked just like Hadley at that age. He was toast. "Ok, ok, I see what's happening here."

Maddie giggled and danced as he rolled into the song. He kept his focus on the kid, on her effervescent happiness that was absolutely worth whatever crap Brax and Jonah would sling his way.

When he'd finished, Maddie clapped and bounced. "Again!"

"Another time, Munchkin," Cayla told her. "As he said, we're about to get to work. Say 'thank you.'"

Maddie waved him down, so Holt crouched to her level. She pressed a smacking kiss to his cheek. "Thank you!"

This kid.

"You're welcome."

As she scampered back down the hall, he rose, rubbing at the little ache in his chest.

"Wow. I've really got to make it to karaoke night next time," Mia observed.

Cayla was looking at him with amusement.

"You know she's going to be like a dog playing an endless game of fetch now, right?"

"Yeah. I'm familiar." And Holt chose not to think too hard about the fact that he didn't mind it. "Okay then, where do you want to start?"

"Oh, my goodness! Look how much y'all got done today!"

Cayla joined her mom in a survey of the little house. With everyone's help, the entire place had been primed and the first coat of cheery butter yellow applied. "We're so close. Thanks for staying with Maddie tonight, so I can stay late and finish."

Brax, Mia, and Jonah had packed up half an hour ago to head out to other obligations, but Holt was still at it, so Cayla made introductions. "This seemingly tireless saint of a helper is Holt Steele. Holt, this is my mother, Donna Black."

"Ma'am." He nodded a greeting and tipped back a fresh bottle of water.

Cayla tore her eyes away from the ripple of his throat as he swallowed. Why on earth should that be sexy?

Donna split an appraising look between them, clearly wondering about the nature of their relationship. "Nice to meet you. You're one of the bakers from across the street?"

"Yes, ma'am."

Maddie tugged at her sleeve. "Mimi, did you know Holt can sing Maui?"

"Can he, now?"

"He *can*. He knows *all* the words."

With suitable sobriety, Donna nodded. "That's very impressive." But it didn't save Cayla from The Eyebrow.

Lord have mercy, her child was digging all kinds of holes today.

Better to quash whatever ideas that put into her mother's head.

"Aren't you ready to call it a day, Holt?"

"I'm sticking around to help." As if to emphasize the point, he just picked up the roller and began to apply the next coat.

Flustered, Cayla scrambled. "Oh, you don't have to do that. We're so much further along than I thought we'd be."

He just leveled those implacable blue eyes on her. "I am not leaving you here alone at night. You stay, I stay."

Her mouth fell open, but nothing came out. What the hell could she say to that?

Donna had no trouble stepping in. "Oh, I have to tell you that puts my mind at ease. I know things have been quiet since the—" She glanced down at Maddie. "—trouble across the street, but a mother worries."

Trouble. That was one word for the showdown a few months back when some nut job nearly killed Mia during the renovation of the bakery building. Thank God Brax had showed up in time to stop him.

"I'll see her home safe, ma'am."

Her mom beamed a considerably warmer smile in his direction. "Thank you, Holt. And you should come by for Sunday dinner some weekend."

Cayla fought not to drop her face into her hands again. Now her mom was playing matchmaker? Or was she just lining him up for an inquisition to determine if he was worth matchmaking?

"That'd be nice. You just let me know when, and I'll bring dessert."

Don't I get a say in all this?

Evidently deciding that Cayla's opinion wasn't needed, her mother just rolled on. "Excellent. I'm sure we'll been in touch." Taking Maddie's hand, she started for the door. "We're gonna go on, so y'all can get back to work." The eyebrow waggle she aimed in Holt's direction suggested she thought Cayla should do something else that had nothing to do with work.

Ignoring that, Cayla picked up another roller herself. "Thanks, Mama."

"Mimi! Can we read *Ice Cream Soup* before bed tonight?"

"We can probably make that happen." Donna shut the door behind them, cutting off the fresh ramble Maddie started about her day.

Cayla let out a slow breath and with it some of the fierce hold she had on the mask she wore, pretending she had everything together. It had been a long ass day, and she was so damned tired. She'd be tireder yet before it was through. Par for the course. But maybe they'd at least get done with this main room.

Nerves trickled in again as the silence settled. Without the buffer of other people, they were harder to ignore, so she focused on the painting, starting on the wall opposite him. She didn't know what they were doing here. Why was he helping? Why was he entertaining her daughter? Because he wanted to be friends? She'd certainly never had a friend like him. Friends didn't make her belly swoop and her skin heat with a look. Maybe she was just viewing this through the lens of her undeniable attraction, wishing and hoping against her better judgment for something that wasn't even there. Holt Steele was a good man. She'd known a few in her life, but none had been interested in her. Why should that change now?

Despite the attraction, the silence between them was easy. He wasn't hard to just be with. There was no implicit demand in his presence, no role he seemed to expect her to play. So she painted, soaking in the quiet that was rare as hen's teeth in life with a five-year-old. By the time they reached the end of their respective walls and turned onto the one between them, some of the sharp edges from this morning had smoothed out a little.

"I appreciate you sticking around."

"No problem."

A little of the disquiet returned. "Is there reason to worry that someone is lurking around?" God knew, she worried about that enough on her own for reasons that had nothing to do with her business neighbors.

"No. I didn't mean to worry you. I'm just being cautious." His gaze settled on her face for a long moment before he moved away to refill the paint tray. "You can tell me no, and I'll leave it alone, but just in case you didn't want to mention it in front of everyone else, I'll ask again... what's wrong?"

Her heart thudded. "Why do you think something's wrong?"

"You're a lousy liar." The statement was made without malice or accusation. "Something's upset you. If you don't want to talk about it, that's fine. I'm not big on talking either. But in case you do, I've got a good ear."

She dipped her roller and applied it to the wall in front of her, finding that she wanted to tell someone. "I got a letter from my ex-husband yesterday."

"Is that unusual?"

"Unfortunately, no. He can't get to me any other way from prison, so he sends letters."

"Prison?" With that one word, she heard him snap to attention, the protector instantly assessing a threat.

She blinked, belly swooping with dread this time. "I can't believe I just said that out loud. Nobody here knows. Please don't tell anyone."

"Of course not." His ready assurance of discretion eased the tension.

Cayla could feel him waiting, but despite his obvious,

vibrating need to know, he didn't pressure her. She debated with herself. No one here knew but her mother, and even she wasn't aware of the letters. Maybe it would be good to tell someone the story. Holt claimed to want to be friends. If he could hear this ugliness and still wanted that, it would be a blessing to have him in her corner. And if he didn't, well, she was pretty sure he'd still keep his mouth shut if for no other reason than he wasn't a gossip.

"I met Arthur when I was a senior in college."

"Arthur?" Holt didn't quite manage to hide the sneer in his tone.

Cayla's lips twitched. "Arthur Bronson Raynor, III."

"Sounds like a pretentious Upper East Side accountant."

She snorted. "Oh, he'd hate that description. Despite the name, he didn't come off as pretentious. He was... magnetic. Older than me by almost a decade. I was flattered by his interest and primed to be swept off my feet. I was such a cliche. My dad died when I was little, so I guess I was always looking for that strong male influence. We were married in six months, and I ended up not graduating. What did it matter if I got my degree? He could afford to support us both, and he wanted to shower me with this lavish lifestyle. It felt like I'd found my very own prince charming."

"You're divorced, so I'm guessing it didn't stay that way."

"No. I was so bespelled at the beginning, I didn't realize how he was slowly, systematically cutting me off from home. From my family and friends. Our life was in San Francisco. It was a long way from Tennessee, and I had obligations and duties as his wife. I wanted to please him. So I stopped coming home. Stopped returning calls and emails. I told myself I'd catch up later. After he'd impressed this client or achieved that goal. But later never came."

From six feet away, she could feel Holt's coiled tension. "Did he hurt you?" The question came out deadly calm, almost conversational, but Cayla sensed the potential for violence beneath. Here was a man who protected women and children —the innocent—because it was the right thing to do.

"Not physically. It was all about control. Psychological manipulation. I'm not sure if it would have escalated if I'd stayed."

"What made you leave?"

"I found out I was pregnant. And I could just see how he was going to make excuses and say we didn't need my mother's help or whatever. How he'd cut me off further. I didn't tell him about the baby. I'd already made up my mind to go when I found out about the identity theft."

"Identity theft? Yours?"

"No. He had a home office. It wasn't where he did most of his work, but everything was kept on cloud drives, and he was more careless with his passwords than he should've been. I hadn't set out to snoop. My laptop got the blue screen of death, so I went in to use the computer in his office, and I found out that he'd committed mass scale identity theft. Some for himself. A lot more for some really powerful people. The lavish lifestyle we led had been built largely off ruining the lives of children and the elderly." Even now, it disgusted her how blind she'd been. Shoving away the sense of failure, she continued, "So I gathered everything I could find, and I took it to the FBI. He was arrested, convicted of I don't know how many counts of fraud, and sent to prison."

"Shit. That's incredibly brave."

"It didn't feel brave. It felt... necessary. And not anywhere near enough for all the lives he destroyed." She shrugged, as if the twitch of her shoulders would dislodge the weight that had settled there. "I came home after that. Didn't tell a soul the truth other than my mother, and I started over. I divorced him after he was incarcerated. That took forever."

"Does he know about Maddie?"

"I'd have kept her existence from him entirely if I could, but it had to be disclosed as part of the divorce proceedings. He's never met her. Never even seen a photo. She's not his in any way. If he ever got his hands on her, he'd break everything bright and beautiful about her. I will do anything to stop that from happening."

"You keeping tabs on him?"

"Yeah. I check in every couple of months. And he sends letters about as often." Just enough to remind her that he remembered. That he was waiting.

"Threatening?"

"Not overtly. Xander's got copies of all of them, just in case." Though the sheriff had been clear that there wasn't much that could be done based on vague allusion. As long as Arthur stayed in prison, it didn't matter. He couldn't do anything from where he was.

"Good."

They lapsed back into silence.

Feeling exposed and more than a little uncomfortable with her admissions, she flashed a self-deprecatory smile. "Anyway, that is the sad and tragic tale of my complete crap taste in men, and the reason I've been single ever since."

"Not entirely sad and tragic. You got Maddie. She's amazing."

Cayla stared at him. He got it. He so clearly understood that her daughter was her greatest joy. "Yeah, she is. There's none of her father in her."

"Being a sperm donor doesn't make someone a father."

This guy was just racking up the points left and right.

"True enough. You're really great with her." The words slipped out before she could stop them. She backpedalled, trying to mitigate the damage. "I don't say that because I'm auditioning replacements. It's just an observation."

One corner of that usually serious mouth quirked up. "I like kids."

"How is it you're so good with them? I wouldn't have thought a life in the Army would've predisposed you to be."

"I raised my baby sister."

She waited for him to elaborate, but he just turned back to the wall. Accepting that maybe that topic was off-limits, she did the same and changed the subject. "How are the plans for the opening going?"

"We're still deciding on a date for the grand opening. But we're gonna do a limited-hour soft opening to test recipes out starting next week."

"That's awesome! I have to confess, I'm surprised y'all are actually going with Bad Boy Bakers for the name. I was half joking when I suggested it."

He jerked those big shoulders. "You weren't wrong. It's hooky. And we need whatever help we can get to get the place off the ground. If that means we get a chunk of traffic that wants to check us out like slabs of beef while we get baked goods in their hands, so be it. We're cheap advertising. After that, the food will speak for itself."

"You know, I know a little bit about bootstrapping marketing. I'm happy to help with that in exchange for the free labor y'all have been kind enough to offer."

"We're friends. Friends help each other without expectation of repayment. That said, we know we can't just rely on 'If we bake it, they will come.' So we'll take whatever marketing help we can get."

Relieved to have something to offer, Cayla smiled. "Then consider it a deal. Friend."

3

Holt's skin prickled with anticipation. It was nearly go time.

"Menu board?" Holt asked.

Brax slid the sign with the day's offerings and prices scrawled in block print onto the hooks on the side wall. "Locked and loaded."

"POS system?"

Jonah stabbed a few buttons, causing the cash register drawer to pop out. He shoved it back in. "Up and running and full of change."

Holt bent to slide the last tray of blueberry muffins into the display case that stood on the site of the original scarred wooden bar. The streusel topping glittered like edible diamonds. They looked good beside the orange cranberry scones and the apple cinnamon oatmeal bars. Brax had filled the other side of the case with gleaming, buttery pastries. The shelves on the wall behind them were loaded with baskets full of Jonah's boules and baguettes. It wasn't the full array of what they'd be offering, but it was a good start to begin testing their market and seeing what would sell.

He looked around the bakery in satisfaction. Beyond the counter sat a half dozen four-top tables they'd built themselves from reclaimed pallet board. More seating was available on stools beneath the narrow counter ledge wrapping three walls of the front. Large picture windows had been put in on the left and right, giving a view to the mountains beyond and a glimpse of the porch that wrapped around three sides and provided more seating.

No one who hadn't seen it before would realize that the building had once housed The Right Attitude, the sketchy-beyond-belief bar that had been owned by Jonah's late father. Mia had done one hell of a job on the renovation. Holt loved the rustic industrial vibe she'd given them. The shiplap walls and iron accents lent a masculine feel to what otherwise might have been an unnecessarily feminine space. But there was no mistaking that this was a place of men.

Each of them wore one of the custom t-shirts they'd had designed with the company logo, a military-style shield with a whisk and rolling pin crossed like swords to honor where they'd come from.

Jonah, usually the most optimistic of their trio, cracked his knuckles and rolled his shoulders in a rare betrayal of nerves.

"You okay, brother?" Holt asked.

He braced his hands on the counter and let out a long, slow breath. "What if they don't come? What if I dragged you both down here, and we all invested all this money in this place, and they don't come?"

"They're gonna come," Brax insisted.

"But what if we didn't do enough?"

Holt laid a hand on Jonah's shoulder and squeezed. "That's what all this is for. The word went out on social media about the soft opening. Cayla saw to that. It's spinning around town. This is just a test to try out different recipes, see how things go over. If it doesn't work well, we've got time to adjust before the official opening."

He sucked in another breath and nodded. "Okay. We can at least count on my mama and her friends for sure. That will probably make a decent dent in today, even if nobody else shows up."

"Then let's do this thing," Brax insisted.

They all bumped knuckles, and Holt went to unlock the heavy front door.

People were *everywhere*. The parking lot was already nearly full, with more vehicles pulling in. A line of customers snaked through the cars, with people chatting in clusters, enjoying the gorgeous spring weather while they waited. He recognized some of the deputies from the Sheriff's Department, along with a few of the other military vets he'd met since coming to town. But there were more, so many more. And the women. They made up the lion's share of the crowd. Evidently, the whole Bad Boy Bakers thing really did hit that target audience.

"Holy shit," he muttered.

Mia and her crew were the first to notice the open door. She let out a two-fingered whistle and waved them forward. "Morning, Holt. Hope you guys baked a lot because we showed up starving."

He stepped back and people streamed in, the babble of their voices echoing off the wood and filling the building with life. They were officially open for business. Taking a position behind the counter, he found himself across from Brick Hooper, Mia's foreman.

Short and thick, with warm, sepia skin and close-cropped black hair, Brick's gaze was hopeful as he scanned the case. "I was hopin' y'all'd have some of those sourdough breakfast sandwiches y'all brought to the job site."

"Not today, unfortunately, but they are still on the menu for consideration when we get fully up and running. If you're feeling something savory, why don't you try these sausage and cheddar hand pies?"

"I do like sausage. Let me have one of those and one of those bar things as somethin' sweet for later."

"You got it." He bagged up Brick's order and rang him up before circling back to the other end of the display cases to do it all over again.

Spotting Jonah's mother, Rebecca, on the other side, he broke into a grin. "Hey, Mama Ferguson. What can we get you this morning?"

She beamed back at him. "The way to my heart today is muffins. I'll take four. I promised Candice I'd bring something back to the shop since she couldn't get away. But I had to come check on my boys."

"We sure appreciate it."

They didn't yet have the boxes they'd ordered. Holt made a mental note to check on that when things slowed down and carefully loaded the muffins into two bags so they wouldn't get squashed. She paid for her purchase and slipped around the counter to give all three of them big hugs before disappearing.

Customers kept coming. He'd helped a dozen before he realized he was looking down the queue for a familiar blonde head. With all the work Cayla had done helping them get the word out, he figured she'd be one of the first to show up. That little pang he felt at not seeing her wasn't disappointment. It was just indigestion. Or something.

But a different familiar face stood out in the throng. Holt recognized the woman as one of the friends Cayla had been out with at karaoke night. Tall and slim, with skin the shade of warm, rich caramel and a riot of red-brown curls, she had her hand linked with another woman with fair cheeks and a short cap of brown hair that reminded him of Audrey Hepburn.

As they reached the front of the line, her bright white smile widened. "Well, if it isn't the king of karaoke."

"I see my reputation precedes me. I remember seeing you there that night, but I'm afraid you have me at a disadvantage."

"I'm Astrid Corneau, and this is Lena."

"Nice to meet you, ladies. I'm Holt Steele. What can I get you?"

"A blueberry muffin for me, one of those gorgeous scones for my wife, and the inside scoop on when you're gonna ask our girl Cayla out."

Holt went brows up. "Come again?"

"Oh, don't play coy. We all saw you two up there."

He was grateful for all the training he had on resisting interrogation. It kept him from dropping his mouth open like an idiot fish. But really, what did he expect? He'd flirted with her on stage, in front of probably half the town. Of course they'd assume he was interested. And he was. He was just... still trying to talk himself out of it. Not that he was having the slightest bit of luck on that front, and his actions certainly hadn't done a thing to dispel the idea that he was into her.

"Well, now, I don't sing and tell." As Astrid and Lena laughed, he bagged up their order and rang them up.

"We're keeping an eye on you, Sergeant Studly."

"Noted." Holt counted himself lucky when they left without further comment. But his relief was short-lived because yet another of the bachelorette party crew was next in line.

Zara, the ballsy-as-hell matchmaker who'd asked him to sing with Cayla, stepped up with a wide smile.

"Hey Zara. Can I recommend a chocolate croissant?"

"Already out," Brax put in.

"Oh." Holt glanced down at the display cases, which were looking pretty sparse. "What about an apple cinnamon oatmeal bar?"

"Yes, please."

He added one to a bag. "Anything else?"

"One of those baguettes and a promise that you'll come

back to karaoke night next month. It's so much more fun when people who can actually sing get up there."

"Thanks. We'll see."

Her smile turned sly. "I can promise to drag Cayla out to sing with you."

"She might not want to be dragged." After what she'd told him about her ex, he wasn't about to be pushing her into anything. Especially when he didn't know what he wanted himself. Well, that wasn't entirely true. He *wanted* her. But he wasn't looking for more than that. He was still getting his new life together. So was she. A casual affair or friends with benefits didn't fit into the life of the kind of single mom she was. He respected that. So he'd be her friend. That was all.

"Oh, I don't think it would take that much convincing," Zara opined.

Rather than reply, Holt gave her the total. She just shot him a knowing smile and took her breakfast.

The morning rolled on, but Cayla didn't show. He couldn't help but wonder where she was. She probably had a client meeting or had to make a trip to a vendor. As the crowd finally began to thin enough that they could breathe, he stepped outside under the auspices of getting a little fresh air. If he happened to glance across the street to see if her car was at the office, well, it was in front of his face, wasn't it? The Camry was parked in front of the little porch. She was probably busy. Maybe he'd just take a little something over. If there was anything left.

Inside, he surveyed the decimated trays. There was a single muffin remaining. Before anyone else could grab it, Holt bagged it up and tucked it away.

"You hiding our wares?" Jonah asked.

"Nope. Just saving it for Cayla. Thought it would be a nice thank you for her help with getting the word out about today on social media. Obviously it worked."

"I'll say. The apple oatmeal bars were a little slow, but every-thing more or less flew off the shelves." Brax made a notation on the pad he carried. "If we continue to get crowds like this, we're going to need to majorly bump up our inventory. I have one more batch of bars and another of muffins about to come out of the ovens."

"We're still a novelty. No guarantee they'll come back," Jonah said.

"Oh, son, we'll come back." The rusty voice came from a grizzled old dude in an ancient Army jacket at one of the four-tops. He sat with a trio of equally old guys who all had the look of former military. There was nothing left but crumbs on their plates.

Jonah smiled. "Think so?"

"Know so," said one of the others.

"But you really gotta get some coffee."

Holt exchanged a look with his friends. "We'll add it to the list."

Cayla let the measuring tape snap back and carefully sketched out the main space of the office. Once she'd cleaned up and refinished it, the sideboard she'd snagged at the flea market last month would go perfectly along that entry wall, with some kind of cute display that included business cards and portfolios of the events she'd put together. The used file cabinets she'd scored had already been wrestled back to the tiny bedroom she was using as an office. Clients wouldn't be back there, so there was no sense wasting a lot of time on pret-tying them up. Maybe if she got motivated, she'd repaint them or add some contact paper to cover up the rust spots. For now, her efforts needed to go toward the public spaces.

Wandering toward the front window, she mused over

whether she should be on the lookout for a secondhand sofa and chairs for client meetings or if a dining table would be better. The sofa would be cozier but having a table to spread out photos and samples might be more practical. And probably a table and chairs would be kinder to her budget. She'd keep an eye out for a used set she could spiff up. Then she could put up a large magnetic marker board along that wall to capture ideas. Yes, it could work. She made more notes, enjoying the bump of pleasure she always felt at making plans and seeing the path to bringing them to fruition.

Her eyes shifted to look out the window, up the hill toward the bakery. There was an area she didn't know how to make plans and certainly couldn't see the path forward. She'd missed the soft opening this morning. But they'd had an in-service day at school, and she'd had to sort out what to do with Maddie so she could make her meeting with a prospective client who wanted to plan an engagement party for her daughter. Thank God for Mama. She'd taken Maddie to work at the library.

Guilt prickled. She'd been leaning on her mother an awful lot lately. Not that Donna ever seemed to regret it. She adored her granddaughter, and Lord knew the feeling was mutual. But Cayla felt as if she was abusing the help. Like she was supposed to be able to juggle everything on her own. Maybe she just wanted to be able to give that example to her daughter so Maddie wouldn't be sucked in by some manipulative, controlling, sociopathic asshole when she grew up. Then again, wasn't the lack of a strong male figure in her own life part of how she'd been taken in by Arthur?

Cayla's gaze fixed on the flash of silver tin roof—all she could see of the bakery from here. Her thoughts were full of Holt. She'd meant what she'd told him last week. She wasn't auditioning a replacement father for Maddie. But it was hard to see how good he was with her and not wish for someone like that in her child's life. And it was hard for the woman to look at a man like him and not remember exactly how long it had been since she'd been touched.

Not that he was volunteering. Despite the behavior that might easily be construed as interest in something more, the word he kept tossing about was friends. She valued her friends, even if she seldom got to spend the kind of time with them she'd like. And as Holt's friend, she'd promised him she'd be at the opening. Feeling guilty, she pulled out her phone and thumbed out a text.

Got tied up with a client meeting this morning. How did the soft opening go?

Those three little dots began dancing a few moments later.

Holt: **It went great. They wiped out everything.**

Cayla had no idea how much the guys had made, but that definitely sounded like a success. She tapped a reply. **Everything?**

He sent back a picture of the completely empty bakery cases. Only a few crumbs remained on the trays.

Cayla: **Wow. Now I really regret missing it.**

Again with the bubble indicating he was typing a response.

Holt: **No worries. I saved you a little something.**

Oh, that was so sweet of him. She wondered what he'd snagged for her and if he'd specifically grabbed something that he'd baked. What did it say if he did?

As the front door opened, she smiled. "And what good deed did I do to merit personal delivery?"

But it wasn't Holt who came through the door.

It was Arthur.

Cayla froze, as if staying still would somehow make her invisible. She was dreaming. Caught up in some kind of nightmare inspired by the latest letter. Because there was no way that her ex-husband was standing here in her office space. And if it was a nightmare, she could wake up.

Oh please God, let me wake up.

"Hello, Cayla."

At the sound of that voice, smooth and cultured and so intimately familiar, fear bloomed hard and fast, an invasive vine twining through her body, squeezing, squeezing, until she was rooted, quivering, to the spot.

Why was he here? *How* was he here? He should have been serving multiple sentences in prison.

Thank God, thank *God*, she hadn't brought Maddie to work with her. Nothing was more important than protecting her child.

Swallowing against the cotton in her mouth, Cayla had to fight to keep her voice steady. "What are you doing here?"

His lips curved into a smile that didn't reach his eyes. They were so cold, so flat. Had they always been so lifeless, or was this a product of prison?

"Not expecting to see me? I had good luck with my last appeal. All my convictions were overturned, and I'm a free man, ready to take back my life."

Cayla heard what he didn't articulate. *Ready to take back my wife.* Because she'd been a possession to him, and the legalities of a divorce—particularly one he'd fought tooth and nail— wouldn't change that in his eyes. Blood roared in her ears, and she struggled to breathe. Desperate, she slid her thumb over the face of her phone, still open to Holt's text, hoping beyond hope she managed to hit record for a voice text.

"You can't be here, Arthur." She moved her thumb again and felt the faint vibration of a text sending. She didn't dare take her eyes off him to check to see if she'd recorded anything at all. She could only pray that Holt got the message and understood it for the SOS it was.

That false smile didn't waver. "I'm just coming to check in on my wife."

"Ex-wife." Even as she said it, she could see the flare of temper in those cold, cold eyes.

"I'm also here to meet my daughter."

Pure, abject terror washed through her. She'd do literally anything to keep him from Maddie. "You aren't getting anywhere near my daughter."

"Come now, there's no need for this hostility. I have a right to get to know my child."

Before she could formulate a reply, the door opened again and Holt stalked through. Cayla met his eyes over Arthur's shoulder. Here, too, was chilled fury. But it was so very different from her ex-husband's. This was a warrior ready for battle, and at the sight of him, the grip of panic eased a fraction. She knew on a deep, instinctive level that he'd keep her safe.

Stepping past Arthur, Holt slid an arm around her. The warmth of his touch melted some of the ice in her veins. "Who's this?"

Desperately grateful for his presence, and for the fact that he was a big, imposing badass, Cayla leaned into him, as much because her legs didn't want to support her anymore as to play along. "This is Arthur. My ex-husband. He was just leaving."

The smile had faded, his pale gold eyes taking in Holt's proprietary arm around her. Something ugly seemed to slither beneath the bland expression on his face. "I'm not here to cause trouble. I'm just here to see my daughter. And who, exactly, are you?"

Before she could come up with any kind of response, Holt was speaking. "I'm her current husband, and you have no rights here."

Struck dumb by this announcement, Cayla could only watch Arthur. For a few seconds, the bland expression crumpled, those glacial eyes sparking with something vicious before he got himself under control again. "We'll see what the courts have to say about that. Be seeing you soon, sweetheart."

4

Holt glared after the departing man, wishing he had sufficient justification to use the many lethal skills at his disposal. Pressed tight to his side, hand fisted in his t-shirt, Cayla trembled, but she didn't say a word. Even if every cell of his body hadn't recognized Raynor as a threat, that would've done it. Allowing the man to walk away was taking all his considerable control. But he'd be no good to her behind bars for what he considered justifiable homicide.

At the sound of a car door slamming, Cayla jerked away.

Holt opened his mouth to say—well, he didn't have any idea what—about the husband thing, but she was racing for the back of the house. He trailed her down the short hall, finding her in the little office, snatching up her purse. Her eyes were wild and desperate.

"Maddie! I have to get to Maddie."

She was way too rattled to drive. "Cayla, you need to wait."

Hysteria edged her voice, raising it an octave. "I'm not going to *wait!* That monster is walking free. I have to get to my daughter!"

Stepping into the office to block her path, he took her

gently by the arms. "Cayla, honey, that asshole could be hanging around nearby somewhere just waiting for you to lead him right to her."

What little color had come back into her cheeks leeched away again, and Holt cursed himself. "He doesn't know where she is. Not yet. We have some time. You need to take a few minutes to calm down. If she sees you this upset, it'll freak her out. Now, where is she? School?"

"No. No, it was a teacher workday. She's at the library with my mother."

Thank Christ. Raynor wouldn't have had any way of knowing that, so even if he went by the school, she wouldn't be there. "Okay, you're gonna call your mom, talk to Maddie to reassure yourself she's okay. I'm sending one of the guys over to be with them. Let's confirm where they are. All right?"

After a long moment, she nodded and collapsed back against the desk. She sucked in several breaths before dialing. "Mama? Are you and Maddie still at the library?" The instant sag of her shoulders was answer enough. "I need to talk to her for a minute. No, it's not okay. I'll explain, but I need to talk to her first."

He started to step out to call the guys, but she reached out and snagged his hand. He curled his fingers tight around hers, offering her whatever strength he could while he sent a text with his request to the group chat with his partners.

Need one of you to head to the library ASAP for guard duty on Maddie and Cayla's mom. Will explain later.

"Hi, baby. Are you having fun at the library with Mimi?" She'd schooled her voice to something approximating normal, but there was still a tremor beneath.

At Maddie's happily chattered reply, Cayla closed her eyes.

"That's good to hear. *Mr. Popper's Penguins* is one of my favorites, too. Of course, we can start it at bedtime."

Holt's phone dinged with the reply from Brax. **En route.**

"I miss you, too. Can you put Mimi back on? Uh-huh. I love you too, baby. So much." Her grip on his hand was so tight. "Hey, Mama."

He was close enough now to hear Donna's reply.

"Cayla, what is going on?"

"I don't—" Cayla cut herself off, as if the situation were so bad, she didn't even know where to start. Tears slid down her cheeks, and rage ignited in Holt's veins.

The son of a bitch had made her cry. He'd pay for that.

Tugging Cayla into a full hug, he took the phone from her hand. "Donna, this is Holt Steele. I need you to stay calm and keep your granddaughter close. Arthur Raynor is out of prison and is here in Eden's Ridge."

"Oh my God. How?"

"I don't know, but I can assure you, I'm finding out. My business partner, Brax Whitmore, is on his way to the library to keep watch over both of you. You need to make arrangements to get off work early, if possible, and head on home. Brax will stay with you. I'm here with Cayla, so she's not by herself. We're going to figure out the next steps and let you know."

"Okay. Maddie, baby, come here. Holt, we'll talk soon."

"Yes, ma'am."

Holt hung up and laid her phone on the desk so he could wrap Cayla closer. She was shaking again, hard enough her teeth chattered.

"H... how can this happen?"

"We'll get to the bottom of it. But I need you to tell me everything that happened. Everything he said. Can you do that?"

Her voice was muffled as she told the story against his chest.

"He said he'd had good luck with his last appeal. That all his convictions were overturned, and he was a free man. I don't understand. They said they had all the evidence they needed.

How could it be overturned when he's already been serving his sentence?"

It was a damned good question. "I've got a guy who can dig into it. But let's talk about the more immediate issue. Will he come after Maddie, or is he all talk?"

Cayla lifted her head, and the look in her eyes shredded his gut. "Oh, he'll come after her. Not out of any kind of love or desire to have a relationship with his child, but because he'll believe she belongs to him. The same way he thinks I still do."

"You're divorced."

"That doesn't matter to a man like him. He views me as his property. And I have no idea what he's going to do with what you threw out. What were you thinking, claiming to be my husband?" Baffled consternation knit her brows together.

He hadn't been thinking. Not really. He'd already been walking over when he'd gotten her voice text. From that point, the only thing in his head was getting to Cayla, protecting her in whatever way he could. And when he'd walked in and seen her there, face sheet white, his immediate instinct had been to shield what was his. But he hadn't had a chance to process what the hell that meant, and he didn't think Cayla would appreciate that just now.

"That it might intimidate him. It seemed like a good idea in the heat of the moment."

She pulled away, swiping at her face. "Yeah, well, you basically just waved a red flag at a very smart and calculating bull. He's not going to just let this go because I allegedly belong to someone else. He'll never acknowledge that claim. I was his first, and as far as he's concerned, I'm his always. I only felt safe because he was behind bars and was supposed to stay there for a good long while. Now I... I don't know what to do."

Her shoulders shook as the tears fell harder.

Holt curled his hands into fists, desperate to *do* something. "He's not going to get to either of you. I swear it."

"How can you promise that?"

His brain spun, considering and rejecting scenarios. If Raynor sued for some kind of custody of Maddie, being caught out in a lie would hardly be in Cayla's favor. And even if he didn't, would they even be safe in their own home? The man she'd described wouldn't let a piece of paper like a restraining order stop him—if they could even get one. They needed protection on site. Both of them. And there was one obvious solution.

"Marry me."

HER BABY WAS SAFE, and Cayla didn't think she could ever let her go again. Not so long as her father was walking free.

Maddie, however, had other ideas. After returning Cayla's hug, she squirmed. "Can I watch 'Honey, Honey,' Mama?"

The grown-ups had so much to discuss that these little ears didn't need to hear. If that meant indulging her daughter's love for ABBA, so be it. "Sure, Munchkin."

"Yay!" Maddie wriggled free and made a beeline for the living room, bringing back the remote to Donna's smart TV.

Cayla pulled up YouTube and navigated to the curated playlist she'd made of all the musical numbers from the movie version of *Mamma Mia!*. If Maddie didn't get hungry, it would buy them about half an hour to figure out what the hell they were doing next. She was already singing—or rather, bellowing —along with the opening number as Cayla joined the others in the kitchen.

Holt's gaze flicked toward the living room. "*Mamma Mia!*?"

"Just the musical numbers. She's still too young to understand the context of the story, and she really, *really* loves ABBA."

"So, what exactly is going on?" Brax asked. "I'm happy to

help play bodyguard, but I'd like to know what I'm guarding against."

Knowing Maddie was safe in the next room, Cayla was calm enough to plan. She could do this. Planning was what she did best. It just rarely involved such drastic prospective consequences.

"Because we don't have time for anything else, the short version is that my ex-husband, who I was instrumental in sending to prison nearly six years ago, apparently had his conviction overturned on an appeal and is out. He showed up at my office this morning and intimated he's coming after custody of Maddie."

Donna pressed a hand to her mouth. "Oh, my God. How on earth did he get out?"

Holt crossed his arms. "I had my buddy check into it. Looks like the appeal won based on some kind of technicality. There'll be a retrial at some point, but he's walking around free until then."

So there'd be a retrial. That was good. That meant there was a good possibility he'd be sent away again. But she couldn't rely on that hope in the meantime.

"He was already good and angry that I divorced him, but he looked practically apoplectic when Holt said we were married."

Donna blinked. "When he said what now?"

Holt shifted, color creeping up the back of his neck. "I kinda barged in and said I was her husband. It seemed like a good idea at the time."

"Oh, my." The look on Donna's face said she found the idea of it romantic.

Cayla couldn't even begin to deal with that, so she just rolled on. "If he were any normal guy, maybe that kind of territory marking would've worked. But he's not. When the lie comes out... I don't know what kind of damage it will do."

Holt met her gaze from across the kitchen. "It's only a problem if it stays a lie."

She stared at him, his blurted proposal at her office coming back. She hadn't responded in the moment because she'd thought it was just another impulsive remark, like claiming to be her husband when faced with the threat of her ex. But she'd learned enough of this man over the past few months to understand he wasn't impulsive. "You were *serious?*"

"Think about it. For the foreseeable future, you two need a bodyguard, at the very minimum. If he goes for custody, how much better will it look to a judge if Maddie's in a stable family unit, with someone who served honorably in the military, as opposed to a former felon?" He just stood there, calm and composed, as if they were discussing a social media campaign for the bakery instead of life-altering decisions that involved manufacturing a *marriage* out of next to thin air.

"Are you out of your mind?"

"I mean, it's out there, but it's not the craziest idea," Brax put in. "The whole decorated war hero, with the Distinguished Service Cross and Purple Heart, would definitely look better than your ex."

In their interactions thus far, Holt had never said a word about his service, other than to confirm he'd been a Ranger in the Army. At Brax's casual agreement, he fidgeted, as if uncomfortable with the acknowledgment of his heroism. There was probably some appropriate response to that, but damned if Cayla could figure out what it was. Instead, she took another long breath, considering her words.

"Holt, I really appreciate you showing up today and offering to do this, but we can't just get married."

She glanced at Donna, looking for a voice of reason to back her up.

"I think it's a good idea."

Was she the only one here who hadn't sustained some kind of head injury? "Are you kidding?"

Her mother shrugged. "I think Holt's right on all fronts. And I'd certainly feel a whole lot better if he was there to protect you."

So would Cayla, but there was a hell of a lot of difference between having a bodyguard and acquiring a new husband.

If Holt was offended that she didn't just jump at his offer, he didn't show it. His expression remained easy and calm. "Can I speak to you in private for a minute?"

The two of them stepped outside to the back porch, looking out at the slope of lawn that was already popping with blooms of spring color from the ramble of beds along the edges. She'd helped plant most of these beds. Had helped tend them over the years. She wanted her daughter to be able to do the same. And that meant keeping her from her father at all costs. But could she really go through with this lunatic scheme?

"Look, I know you're not looking for a husband. I'm sure after what you went through with Arthur, you're a little gun shy. That's completely understandable. I've got no interest in trying to control you. I'm not doing this to manipulate you into a relationship you don't want. I truly just want to help. To keep both of you safe. Because I partly got you into this mess. And because I don't want to see the light in either of you go out." He took a step closer, those blue eyes searching hers. "Let me help fix it and protect you both in the process."

Cayla wasn't afraid of him. He was a good man. One who'd paid attention and thought of some of the concerns she had swimming somewhere under the disbelief. And it wasn't as if she wasn't attracted to him. Marriage to Holt Steele wasn't a horrifying proposition. Quite the opposite, in fact. And that *was* part of the problem. She didn't know if she could give herself over to the ruse without getting in way over her head.

But her potential for a broken heart didn't matter. Not it if meant keeping Maddie safe.

"I cannot believe I'm asking this." She scooped a hand through her hair. "For how long?"

"As long as it takes." His absolute lack of hesitation told her he was decided, and if she accepted him, he'd see it through, no matter what. She appreciated his conviction.

"Why would you do this?"

He looked away for a moment, scanning the yard, collecting his thoughts. Then he leaned back against the porch rail and absently rubbed at his bad leg. "Because you raised a kid who unhesitatingly kissed the world's biggest booboo instead of shying away like I'm some kind of monster."

Holt's running blade had been a surprise to them both that day they'd stopped by the bakery unannounced. Cayla hadn't known he was an amputee. It certainly didn't slow him down any. In that moment, she'd seen nothing but his unfathomable strength, not a man who was somehow less.

Was that what he thought of himself? What he believed others thought of him? Heart twisting, Cayla stepped into him, cupping his jaw and bringing his eyes back to hers. "There is nothing monstrous about you."

His hands curved around her hips, his eyes filling with heat and something else she couldn't read. They held there, a breath apart, for a dozen heartbeats. She dropped her gaze to his mouth, set in its habitual serious line. The mouth that had starred in more than one of her fantasies.

Holt sucked in a breath, the only sign he wasn't on a completely even keel. "I've spent my career protecting the innocent. I won't let him get to either of you."

Cayla believed him. Absolutely and without reservation. He'd do whatever was necessary to keep Maddie safe. So would she.

"Okay."

He didn't ask if she was sure. He just nodded and tugged her back inside the house.

Donna and Brax both raised their brows in question.

"We're getting married." Cayla uttered the words with a sense of unreality. She hadn't imagined saying them again at all, let alone under these circumstances.

Her mother exhaled a sigh of relief.

"When?" Brax asked.

"As soon as possible," Holt answered.

"Tennessee has no waiting period for marriage licenses. We can do the paperwork and get a license this afternoon. I can call and find out if the judge has any openings for weddings." A courthouse wedding was about as far as it was possible to get from the society extravaganza of her first wedding. Cayla was okay with that.

"You're going to need rings." Donna lifted something off the counter. "They may need sizing, but these were your grandparents' wedding rings."

Emotion rose in Cayla's throat. "Mama."

"They'd approve of you marrying a good man to help protect your little girl. So do I."

Oh hell, she was going to cry again.

Donna clapped her hands. "Now, there's a lot to do and not a lot of time to do it. Brax, you call the courthouse and ask about appointments. If the judge isn't available, Reverend Hodgson owes me a favor. Or we can go on to Johnson City. That might be better to keep this a little quieter. Holt, do you have a suit?"

"Uh, yes, ma'am."

"You'll need to pick it up. Cayla, you're going to need a dress."

As she continued to reel off details and snap out orders, Holt only stared. "Well, I guess you come by it honestly."

5

Holt strode into the rental house he shared with Jonah, Brax on his heels. He had his orders, and they were many, but he intended to execute them without a hitch because Cayla deserved nothing less.

Jonah emerged from the kitchen, a Coke in his hand. "You're back."

"They're getting married." Brax blurted the news with all the enthusiasm of a rich housewife spilling the tea.

Jonah's mouth fell open. "I'm sorry, what now?"

Holt grunted an acknowledgment. "Everything go all right after Brax left?"

"The bakery is fine. I sold every crumb, save for the last two apple cinnamon oatmeal bars because I got hungry. Don't be avoiding the subject. *Married?*"

"Married," Brax confirmed, his tone full of delight and metaphorical popcorn. "The real deal."

Giving them both up as lost causes, Holt headed straight for his room, hauling an enormous duffel bag out of the closet and starting to fill it with the essentials. Before he'd emptied his underwear drawer, his friends were crowding into the room.

Jonah inserted himself between Holt and the bag. "Hold up. How the fuck did you go from some kind of guard duty request on Cayla's mom and daughter to marriage?"

"Cayla's ex-husband is out of prison and threatening to come after Maddie. I'm making sure that doesn't happen." He skirted around his buddy and added a stack of jeans and cargo pants to the bag.

"What kind of threat? Kidnapping? Why aren't we talking about setting up a protection detail instead of matrimony?"

Holt sent up a prayer of gratitude that his friends immediately went to protection, without question. "Because I told the son of a bitch I was her husband."

"Uh... and you did that *why*?"

"Because he's the kind of fucker who thinks a woman is property, and he's more likely to respect the claim of another man than her own boundaries." And if claiming her that way had felt natural as breathing in the moment, Holt didn't have the bandwidth to process it just now. He had gym clothes to pack.

"Okay. So the ex is an asshole Neanderthal. I follow that logic. How did that lead to actual wedding bells?"

Holt headed for the bathroom and began loading his toiletries into a bag as Brax explained.

Jonah didn't look convinced when Holt came back out. "I mean, that's noble and shit, but aren't you the one who said you weren't looking for the whole package deal? That you'd done your time as a caretaker with Hadley?"

Hands braced on the duffel, Holt paused and dropped his head. "Yeah. Yeah, I said that." And he'd meant it. He'd spent all his childhood, all his youth, and a good portion of his adult years being a parent to his baby sister. He'd never resented Hadley, but he'd resented the hell out of the necessity. Out of the fact that his life had never been his own because their mother had never stepped the fuck up. So he hadn't planned on getting married, playing house, doing the family thing. Not now. Maybe not ever.

He turned to face his friends. "None of it mattered a good damn when I walked in and saw her looking like a fucking ghost, while she faced off with her worst nightmare. I can't let her deal with that alone. I won't."

"Again, noble. That's kinda your schtick. But this isn't just a bodyguard detail, man. There are gonna be feelings involved. Already are, on your side, from where I'm standing."

He was getting married in a few hours. It didn't seem worth denying it. "I feel more for them both than I wanted to. Tried to stop. It didn't work. That kid is in here." With one fist, he thumped at his chest. "That alone would've been enough for me to do this. But Cayla. She's..."

There is nothing monstrous about you.

He could still feel her hand against his cheek, see the conviction in those big brown eyes. Without even trying, she'd rocked him to the core, evaporating all his good intentions. He wanted her on levels he hadn't even begun to process. "There's something there, whether I want it or not. So I have to do this. I have to protect both of them."

Jonah's green eyes were sharp, assessing. "And when the threat is past?"

Who the hell knew when that would be? "We'll just have to figure out the rest when we get there. This is the immediate priority."

Jonah and Brax exchanged a look, and he braced for judgment. For them to call him out for being completely nuts. Hell, he knew he was. It didn't change a damned thing.

His buddy nodded. "All right. I guess I'm gonna be digging out my suit. Brax, you've got one floating around in your closet somewhere, right?"

"I'll have Mia grab it. She's not gonna want to miss this."

"Why can't you get it yourself? When is the wedding?"

"They have an appointment with a judge in Johnson City at four-thirty," Brax announced. "Called the courthouse myself."

"*Today?*" Jonah dragged out his phone. "Shit. I'm calling Mom. You need a haircut if you're tying the knot."

Holt dragged a hand through his too-shaggy hair. Yeah, serious occasion called for a proper cleanup. "Appreciate it."

Brax was next. "On a more serious note, what do you need?"

He reviewed his mental list. Clothes and shit for a couple of weeks, at least. He needed to go on and dress for the ceremony here, as he didn't want to mess with a wardrobe change and his prosthesis in a public bathroom. There hadn't been time to discuss the full details of him moving in with Cayla before she'd been whisked off by her mom to do everything on *her* list. He didn't want to just show up with everything he owned tonight. She was facing enough shock and change today. But they'd need to make that transition sooner rather than later.

"I'm packing a bag with the essentials for the night, but I expect I'll need to pack the rest of my stuff to get it ready to move over, quick and quiet. We're keeping this under the radar and not making a big production of the when we got married."

"Yeah, we can help take care of that." Brax waved the details away. "But there are some other things to consider for today."

"Like what?" He had his ID. Cayla had to take care of the lion's share of other requirements for their marriage license since she had to produce her dated divorce decree.

Brax rolled his eyes. "Like the fact that this is your wedding day, man. More importantly, it's *her* wedding day. This is not just about all the technical shit. Yeah, okay, it's unconventional. But any woman deserves something special. And Cayla's a freaking wedding planner. I know there's not a lot of time, and there's no opportunity to put together the kind of shindig she would, but let's figure something out to make this a positive, memorable occasion and not some kind of business transaction, okay?"

Jonah punched Brax in the shoulder. "Marriage has turned you into a hopeless romantic."

"Shut up, asshole. I know what I'm talking about."

That was a fair point. Holt checked his watch. "It's, what, an hour to the courthouse?"

"Yeah, about that."

"I've got an idea. If I hurry, there'll be just enough time."

ARMS OUTSTRETCHED, Maddie twirled until the skirt of her dress belled. "How come we're all dressed up, Mama?"

How come, indeed? In the mad scramble to pull together everything needed for this impulse wedding, there hadn't been a single moment for Cayla to figure out how she was going to explain things to her daughter. She wasn't about to say a word about Arthur. Maddie didn't know about him. Up to now, she hadn't ever really questioned that she had no father. Cayla knew that wouldn't last, especially now that she was nearing the end of her first real year of school. Her classmates would certainly talk about their two-parent households, and eventually that difference would strike her as odd enough to ask about. Cayla still had no idea what to say to those questions.

How did she explain to a five-year-old that her father was a bad man? More, how did she explain the sudden addition of Holt to their household? She hadn't even dated anyone since Maddie was born. She'd been too worried about the prospective impact on her child, worried about her getting confused or attached to someone who might or might not stick around. Maddie was already besotted with him. And while Cayla was certain the feeling was mutual and that he'd remain a part of Maddie's life no matter what, how did she protect her daughter's tender feelings from being crushed when this charade was over, and Holt moved out again?

She ignored the tiny voice asking how she'd protect her own and crouched down to her daughter's level. "You know how I help plan people's big events, like weddings?"

"Uh huh."

"We're here for a wedding."

Maddie screwed up her face in confusion, looking around at the uninspiring civic building that was the courthouse. "But this isn't a church, and there aren't any flowers or music. And you're the only one in a pretty dress."

Cayla glanced down at the pale pink wrap maxi-dress she'd snagged from her closet. She'd bought it as business attire to wear to events she organized. It was hardly bridal, but with the ruffled hem and V-neck, it looked nice, and it was the best she could do on no notice. Working to pin a smile in place, she gave Maddie a little doughboy poke in the belly that had her giggling. "You're in a pretty dress. And anyway, not all weddings are the same. Some happen in churches. Some happen outside. And some are done at courthouses like this one."

Maddie leaned closer and whispered. "Churches and outside are prettier."

Cayla huffed a laugh. "Generally, yes. But there are lots of reasons people might not want to do it that way. Some people prefer a small ceremony instead of the big flashy party." She happened to be one of them. Her wedding to Arthur had been the big, pretentious society wedding, held out in California where almost no one had been seated on the bride's side. She'd told herself it was fine, that she was getting her prince. But she'd ended up with a toad in the end. All the gorgeous dresses and flowers and music in the world couldn't make up for that.

Angling her head, Maddie considered. "That might be okay, as long as there's cake. Do I get to have some cake?"

Oh boy. Basically, nothing about this wedding was going to meet with Maddie's expectations for what weddings should be, and Cayla had no one to blame for that but herself.

"We'll see about that." She sucked in a breath, tucking a lock of Maddie's hair behind her ear. "The thing is, Munchkin, this is my wedding. I'm marrying Holt."

Those brown eyes that were so like hers looked far too serious. "Does that mean Holt will be my daddy?"

She was not prepared for this. Not for the instant and resounding *no* that echoed through her head, nor for the whisper of *yes* that followed. How could she and Holt not have discussed this? Established rules and boundaries and gotten on the same page for how they were going to present this to the very person it was meant to protect?

"Not exactly." Feeling like the worst mother ever, she cupped Maddie's shoulders. "We're gonna play a really big game of pretend. See, Holt really needs a family right now. And since he and I are really good friends, and he likes you so much, I thought we could give him that gift and let him be part of our family for a little while."

She sent up desperate prayers that Maddie didn't ask why, and that she was enamored enough with Holt that she simply went along with it.

"Okay! But there should totally be cake. *Chocolate* cake."

Relief had Cayla's knees wobbling as she stood. "We'll see about getting you some cake."

The echo of approaching footsteps had her turning, expecting to see her mother, who'd been on the lookout for the groom's arrival. Holt strode down the corridor with confidence, his dark blonde hair freshly cut, his beard trimmed neat and close to highlight that square jaw. A charcoal suit hugged his muscular frame like a lover. Cayla's mouth went dry. But it was the flowers in his hands that kicked her heart into high gear.

He came to a stop in front of her, his blue eyes looking faintly uncertain. "Hi."

"Hi."

"I picked up a few things. These are for you." He offered her the bouquet of stargazer lilies. Her favorites.

"Oh!" As stunned pleasure flashed through her, Cayla took them with numb fingers, barely resisting the urge to bury her nose in the blooms, lest she end up with pollen on her face or worse, up her nose. The last thing she needed was a hideous sneezing fit. "Thank you."

"You look beautiful."

"So do you."

Humor replaced uncertainty. "I clean up okay." He shifted his attention to Maddie. "And this is for you." From behind his back he produced a crown of flowers, with trailing ribbons.

Maddie bounced and clapped. "It's a flower princess crown!"

Holt's lips curved in that gentle smile that seemed reserved for her daughter. "It seemed fitting. Pretty princess flowers for a pretty princess."

Cayla pressed a hand to the knot behind her breastbone as he carefully knelt and settled the crown into Maddie's hair. Donna swept in with bobby pins to make sure it stayed put. Only then did she notice the rest of the entourage. Jonah and Brax were likewise dressed in suits. Behind them beamed Jonah's mom, Rebecca. Mia brought up the rear in a bold floral print dress that was so far from the jeans and work boots she habitually wore as a contractor, Cayla had to blink.

Mia stepped around the guys. "I hope you don't mind my crashing. Brax told me what was happening."

"Spousal privilege and all that," he added. "Plus, Holt has us. I wasn't sure if you'd have anybody here for you besides your mom and Maddie."

Moved by his thoughtfulness, Cayla rose to her toes to brush a kiss over his bearded cheek. "Thank you."

Then she hugged Mia, beyond grateful to have one of her girlfriends here. "Thank you for coming."

"I wouldn't have missed this for the world."

"The Black-Steele party?"

They all turned toward the forty-something woman in the cat-eye glasses who stood in the doorway to an office further down the hall.

"Judge McCormick will see you now."

Hands clammy with nerves, Cayla swallowed. This was really happening.

Holt offered her his arm. Shifting the flowers to her other hand, she took it, appreciating the solid curve of muscle beneath her palm. Everything about him was steady, a rock in this sea of insanity.

He covered her hand with his. "Okay?"

She squeezed his arm. "Yeah."

They trooped inside the office, following the receptionist back to Judge McCormick's chambers. It was a large space, furnished in heavy, gorgeously polished wood furniture and leather. Books filled one wall. Legal texts, Cayla assumed. Several potted plants added life and softness to the room.

The judge rose from behind the desk. "Good afternoon."

Maddie bounced straight over to him. "We're getting married today!"

"Maddie!" Cayla hissed.

Judge McCormick only smiled. "Is that right?"

Her daughter nodded vigorously. "And then there's gonna be cake!"

The older man's lips twitched. "That's very important."

"Right?"

Everybody gave up trying not to laugh.

Holt whispered out of the corner of his mouth. "Did you arrange for cake?"

"No, but we'll figure out something. You and your friends are bakers, after all," Cayla whispered back. "Maddie requests chocolate."

"Noted."

They shuffled around, taking their places. As the judge began the ceremony and she stood with Holt's hand in hers, her daughter and her mother by her side, Cayla reflected that this wedding couldn't be more different from her last, and this man couldn't be further from the one she'd wasted her heart on for far too long. No matter how many doubts she had that this was the right move, she knew she was making a better decision in this moment than she had the first go round. So when it was time to slide the ring on his finger and repeat her vows, she made them in a clear and steady voice.

When it was his turn, Holt gently slid her grandmother's ring onto her finger and held there as he repeated his own, those sharp blue eyes never straying from hers. When the judge would have continued, he held up a hand.

"I have something else." Releasing her hands, he reached into his coat pocket. The little silver necklace glinted in the late afternoon sun streaming through the window as he knelt down to Maddie. "This isn't just about me and your mom. It's about you, too. So I wanted you to have something from me today as a token of my promise."

"What is it?" she whispered, eyes big as saucers.

"A bumblebee, because you're mine."

Cayla's throat went thick as he clasped the necklace around her daughter's neck and rose to take each of their hands in his. "'If by my life or death I can protect you, I will.'"

Oh, dear Lord. He was quoting Aragorn in his vows. Viggo Mortensen had nothing on Holt as he looked into her eyes. The man was going to make her swoon.

Judge McCormick cleared his throat. "Well then, by the power vested in me by the state of Tennessee, I now pronounce you husband and wife. You may kiss the bride."

Holy shitake mushrooms. They'd really done it. They'd

really gotten married. And now he was really going to kiss her. In front of an audience.

Cayla's breath caught in her throat as he took a step closer and lowered his mouth to hers. She didn't even have a moment to gasp at the contact because it was already over. A perfunctory brush of lips that might have been quicker than the nervous first kiss she'd gotten in seventh grade from Josh Pattinson.

Holt was already turning away, accepting congratulations and taking Maddie's hand. "I believe someone requested chocolate cake."

And so her new marriage began, not with a bang, but with a quiet whimper.

Hers.

6

"I want a chapter from *Mr. Popper's Penguins*," Maddie announced from the backseat.

Holt watched as Cayla unhooked the five-point harness on the car seat. "We didn't remember to bring it home from Mimi's house, Munchkin."

"But you promised, Mama!" A thread of whine crept into her voice.

Though it had been years, Holt recognized the signs of an overtired kid. And no wonder. After their whirlwind surprise wedding, they'd gone out for a celebratory dinner in Johnson City, followed by the promised chocolate cake. With the hour's drive home, Maddie was crashing on every level. The sigh Cayla tried to muffle told him she wasn't far behind.

"Maddie—"

"I want Holt."

Surprise flashed across Cayla's face before she backed away from the car and made an *after you* gesture.

Holt bent to scoop Maddie up. "You had a really big day, kiddo. And a gigantic piece of cake."

Traces of that cake still streaked one baby-soft cheek.

"I love cake."

He chuckled, following Cayla into the house. "Can I tell you a secret?"

"Yeah."

"My chocolate cake is better."

Maddie's eyes took on an avaricious gleam. "Will you make me one?"

"On two conditions. One, that you do bath and bed without a fuss tonight. And two, that your mom says it's okay."

Maddie folded her hands into prayer position and twisted in his arms toward her mother. "Ohpleaseohpleaseohplease!"

Cayla met his gaze, brows up. "We'll see how you do with bath and bed, and go from there. I'm gonna start the water. Go pick out your jammies."

When she wriggled, he put her down, and she went racing down the hall, presumably to her room.

"Bribery?" Cayla asked.

"It's a classic kid negotiation tactic for a reason. And I did give you full veto rights."

"Smart. You should know that this child is a chocolate fiend. She will do almost anything for Nutella, so use the big guns wisely."

"Understood. While you get her squared away, I'm gonna go grab my bag."

Cayla stared at him for a long moment, clearly only just really absorbing the fact that he'd be living here starting tonight, before nodding and disappearing into the hall bathroom to turn on the water. The day was catching up to them both.

Brax had driven the 4-Runner over, parking it in Cayla's garage before they'd left for the wedding. Holt snagged his duffel from the back and carried it into the house. It was his first real look at the place. He'd never been inside before, and now it would be home. At least for a while.

Just down the street from Mia and Brax's place—at least until they finished the renovation on their dream house further up the mountain—the little bungalow sat on a tidy little lot. The whole place was maybe twelve or thirteen hundred square feet. She'd painted the walls a warm neutral. The kitchen had been done up farmhouse style, with gray green cabinets and butcher-block-style laminate. A round pedestal table and chairs had been painted to match. The living room was full of a comfortable hodgepodge of furniture, including generous baskets that were clearly intended to hold Maddie's plethora of toys and stuffed animals, which were scattered all over. Not knowing if there was a guest room or if he'd be on the sofa, Holt dumped his bag and made a pass through the room to tidy up, figuring it would keep his hands busy and was one less thing Cayla would have to do.

His leg ached from the long day, and he was beyond ready to remove his prosthesis, but that wasn't something he'd be doing out in the open. Cool as Maddie had been when she'd seen it, he didn't want to frighten her by taking it off. And he wasn't exactly excited about doing so in front of Cayla, either. Knowing he was an amputee was one thing. Seeing the scarred ugliness of his stump was something else entirely. She didn't need that in her head.

"Time for bed, Munchkin. Say goodnight to Holt."

She came scampering in, wearing Minnie Mouse pajamas, the ends of her downy soft hair curling from the damp. With dramatic enthusiasm, she threw her arms around his leg—the good one, thank God—and craned her head to look up at him. "I gotta go to bed."

"Me, too," he announced.

"Will you tuck me in?"

Something soft and warm lodged itself in his chest. "You want me to?"

"Yeah." She grabbed his hand and started towing him toward the hall.

Cayla stood staring. "You picked up."

He looked around at the neater room. "Yeah. I'm sorry. Is that a problem? Was that supposed to be her job?"

She shook her head. "No, it's... thoughtful. Thank you."

"C'mon! I wanna show you my room."

Her room was an explosion of purple and plush. More stuffed animals than he'd ever seen in his life were scattered over the bed and floor. A net was suspended from one corner, containing even *more* plushies. Hadley would have had a coronary of pure delight as a kid for all of these.

"Wow."

Maddie bounced onto the bed, diving beneath the covers. Cayla moved in, arranging her menagerie until the little girl was just one sleepy face peeking out. She brushed a kiss over Maddie's cheek. "Goodnight, Munchkin."

"Night, Mama."

Holt stood in the doorway, feeling his chest go tight as he watched the exchange. His mom had never done this. He'd been the one to check Hadley's room for monsters under the bed and in the closet. The one to tuck her in like a burrito so she felt safe enough to sleep. The one to curl up on the floor when she had nightmares.

He jolted as Maddie bolted upright. "Wait! I need Sven!"

Even though he had no idea which stuffie was Sven, Holt looked around. Spotting the reindeer from *Frozen* on the floor at the foot of the bed, he scooped it up. "This guy?"

"Yeah!" She made grabby hands. "Can I have a bedtime song?"

"A bedtime song?"

"Since I'm not getting a story."

"I don't know. What do you think, Sven?" Holt looked at the reindeer, tilting his ear to mime listening to the animal's reply. "Hmm. Okay, I think we can do that."

He cleared his throat and launched into "Reindeer(s) Are Better Than People." Moving closer to the bed, he danced the stuffed animal as he dialed in the voice for its part. Maddie was giggling by the end, wrapping her arms around Sven and tipping her face up for a kiss. He brushed his lips across her brow, lingering for a moment to absorb the scent of bubblegum shampoo and sweetness.

"Don't let the frostbite bite, kid. Goodnight."

Cayla wasn't in the doorway when he turned. The nightlight was on, so he pulled the door until it was just barely ajar and went in search of her. She was down the hall in what he presumed was the master bedroom. It was bright and sunny, as she was, with whitewashed furniture and a very girly floral bedspread. She stood in bare feet at the dresser, still in her dress, looking beautiful and also a little sad as she opened a drawer and scooped out a stack of clothes.

"What are you doing?"

"Making some room for your stuff."

Her gait was a little jerky as she piled clothes in the chair. The moment her hands were empty, they shook. For all her miraculous capacity to roll with things, all the potential ramifications of the day were obviously starting to hit her.

He moved into the room, sliding between her and the dresser and clasping her trembling hands when she reached for another drawer. "It can wait."

Her throat worked. "Okay."

Stepping back, she moved to the door, swinging it closed and turning the lock. The moment her hands went to the tie at her waist, it struck him. This was his *wife*. And she'd apparently resigned herself to doing her marital duty.

Crossing to her in three strides, he stayed her hands. "Don't."

"It's our wedding night. Such as it is."

Because she didn't meet his eyes, he cupped her cheek, wanting to put her at ease. "We both know this isn't a typical marriage. You didn't choose this because you wanted it. You're doing it to protect your daughter. I'm doing it to protect you both. I don't have any expectations here. If we go to bed together eventually, it'll be because you choose it. Because you want me. And if you don't choose that, it's completely okay. You're calling the shots here. Either way, you've been through way too much today, and you need to get some rest."

A potent mix of confusion and relief and something he almost thought was regret swam into her eyes. But she dropped her hands. "We should probably discuss the rest of the details and parameters of all this. There's a lot we left unspoken."

"We will. After you've slept. Is there a guest room?"

"No. I'm sorry. We don't have overnight guests often. Or... ever."

Well, he'd slept under worse conditions.

Because his hands itched to replace hers and tug at that pale pink knot to find what lay beneath, he pressed a chaste kiss to her forehead, much as he'd done to Maddie. "I'll be on the sofa."

Before anything else could override his better judgement, he stepped around her and quietly walked out, closing the door behind him.

SHE'D FORGOTTEN to set up the coffee before bed. Wishing desperately for one of those replicator machines from *Star Trek*, or at the very least, a local coffee shop with a drive-thru, Cayla stumbled down the hall to roust Maddie for the day. If the child didn't dawdle, she could probably manage to brew a couple cups for a travel mug before they had to get out the door for school. Until someone made IV drips of caffeine standard in cars, that would have to do.

"Rise and shine, Sleepyhead." She strode into Maddie's room, crossing to close the window she didn't remember opening last night.

Nothing moved from the vicinity of the bed.

"Come on, kiddo. Time to get up. We're going to be late for school."

There was so much on her plate today. She couldn't remember what all it was, but in her mind's eye, she could see the fully filled pages of her planner. She couldn't afford to be late, not when her business was just starting to really thrive.

Maddie didn't stir. Not surprising. They'd been up well past her bedtime last night. Cayla couldn't quite remember why yesterday had been such a big day or what it was Maddie had been so excited about.

Coffee. Coffee would jumpstart her brain. With that holy grail in mind, she began knocking the mountain of stuffed animals off the bed to dig out her daughter. But there was no sleepy little girl in a heap under the covers.

"Maddie?"

Confused, Cayla checked the bathroom, then the living room. She was running by the time she hit the kitchen.

"Maddie!"

The back door stood open, a trail of muddy footprints leading out to the yard. Footprints far too large to belong to her child. Terror, black and potent, sucked at her heels as she ran out the door, shouting. "Maddie!"

From somewhere beyond the treeline, her daughter cried. "Mommy!"

And the sound of Arthur's chilling laughter floated to her on the breeze. "I always come back for what's mine."

"No! Maddie!"

The touch on her shoulder had her rocketing up, choking on a scream.

"Hey. Hey, it's okay. It was just a bad dream."

Cayla turned toward Holt's low, soothing voice and felt his arms close around her. "He took her. He took her."

"He didn't. Maddie's fine. It was just a dream."

His warmth soaked into her, his solid presence cutting through the panic that followed her out of the nightmare. She held on, fisting her hands in his t-shirt and pressing close to the man who'd vowed to protect them both. His hand tangled in her hair, rubbing tiny circles on her nape that leeched away the fear. But her heart still thundered, her mother's instinct unable to settle without seeing the truth for herself.

"I have to check."

"Okay. Then we'll check." Squeezing her nape once, he eased away, off where he'd sat on the edge of the bed.

Cayla scrambled up, rushing past him, down the hall. Maddie's door was cracked, the glow of the nightlight spilling out. She carefully pushed it open and stepped inside. Her daughter lay sleeping, face squashed to the pillow, one arm hooked around Sven, her knees drawn up so her rump was in the air amid the sea of stuffed animals. The window was closed.

All the tension drained away, relief making her knees weak. On a long sigh, she carefully pulled the door to. Behind her, Holt jerked his head toward the kitchen. She followed him, not questioning how he knew which cabinet held the glasses. He filled one with fresh water and passed it to her. Without a word, she drank it down, wetting her parched throat.

"Better?"

She nodded. Everything was better in this moment, having him here. Not being alone with her fears in the wee hours.

"Wanna talk about it?"

"Not a lot to talk about. After everything that happened, it's not surprising that I dreamed Arthur did exactly what he threatened to do." She shoved a hand through her hair. "I'm sorry I woke you."

"No worries."

Cayla focused in on him, noting that other than the rumpled hair, he looked truly *awake*. He wore a t-shirt and a pair of cut-off sweatpants that showed his prosthesis. Surely he didn't sleep in it. Which meant he'd probably put it back on to come check on her. How fast was he at doing that? She didn't feel like she could ask him.

"Have you slept at all?"

"Some. I'm a light sleeper. Part of my training. You think you can go back to sleep?"

"I don't know. I should try. I've got a full schedule tomorrow. Or today. What time is it?"

"A little after two. C'mon. I'll tuck you back in."

Rather than feeling infantilized by him leading her back down the hall and drawing back the covers, Cayla felt cared for. As she slid beneath the blankets, she thought back to those first few moments after she came out of the nightmare, when his arms had been around her. Everything in her yearned for more of that contact. More of him.

"Holt?"

"Yeah?"

"Will you stay? I just... I'd really like to be held." Embarrassment crawled up her cheeks at the admission, but God, she didn't want to be alone with all her dark thoughts.

He hesitated a moment, and she was on the cusp of giving him an out, when he sat on the edge of the bed and removed his prosthesis. She had questions. How did it happen? Did it still hurt? But she didn't ask, especially as he was very careful to get in so that his good leg was closest to her.

He stretched out an arm, and she cuddled against him, sighing as he closed her into his warm embrace. She hadn't been held by anyone since her divorce, and never like this. All his solid strength surrounded her, blocking out the demons from her past and the echoes of the dream. The slow, steady thump of his heart beneath her palm smoothed her ragged edges.

"Thank you," she murmured. "For everything. I know you didn't choose this either."

He stayed quiet for a long time before finally sucking in a breath. "I'm crazy about your kid. And I've spent most of the past couple months trying not to be crazy about you. Marrying you isn't a hardship, Cayla."

She wasn't up to asking him why he didn't want to feel something for her and wasn't sure he'd answer if she did. It was enough knowing he cared beyond friendship. That this wasn't only about her daughter. She didn't know exactly what she felt for him. Friendship, certainly. Gratitude beyond measure. Lust. There were worse things to base a marriage on. In the intimacy of his embrace in the dark, quiet room, she acknowledged to herself that she wanted a genuine marriage, and everything that went with it, for as long as they lasted.

Cayla thought of what he'd said before about how he had no expectations. That if they went to bed together, it would be because she chose it, because she wanted him. She did want him. Had wanted him for months, even before their lives had become inextricably entwined. He'd been starring in her fantasies almost from their first meeting. Now he was her husband. She could make them real.

She considered rising up, taking his mouth for the kiss she'd wanted as his wife. Seducing and being seduced. But if she pushed for more in this moment, took solace in the pleasure of his body, it felt as if she'd be using him, somehow. That wasn't right. Not when he'd shown her such kindness.

They should take their time, build on the foundation of

friendship, and see where things went. Maybe, just maybe, this crazy scheme could turn into something more. Something real.

Content with the prospect, she settled against the heat of him and pressed a kiss to his shoulder instead. "Goodnight, Holt."

He brushed a phantom kiss to her temple. "Goodnight."

7

H olt woke on the cusp of dawn with an armful of warm, sleep-scented woman and the corresponding morning wood urging him to roll her beneath him for the wedding night he'd denied them both.

Not what she needs, jackass.

Willing away the erection, he turned his face into her hair, enjoying the silky feel of it against his cheek. They didn't have time for a lazy morning. There was work for them both and school for Maddie. But for a few more minutes, he could enjoy this closeness. Sometime in the night, she'd rolled over, and he'd gone with her, wrapping around as big spoon. His palm pressed against the softness of her belly beneath the sleep shirt. Because it itched to slide higher to explore the curve of her breasts and the hard-on wasn't showing any signs of flagging, he eased away, careful not to wake her.

Slipping on his leg, he made his way carefully into her bathroom, checking out the shower situation. A teak bench took up one corner of the small walk-in shower. He could work with that. Retrieving his duffel bag from the living room, he shut himself into the bathroom to clean up and get ready for the day.

Cayla hadn't woken by the time he finished. He didn't know what time she normally got up and wasn't entirely sure what time school started here, but either way, he figured he could get Maddie up and going so she could grab some extra shut eye.

The kid was spread eagled sideways across the bed. At least half the stuff animal mountain had ended up on the floor.

Grinning to himself, Holt gently jiggled the one little foot sticking out from under the covers. "Wake up, Bumblebee. Time to shine."

On an incoherent noise, she yanked the foot away, curling her whole body up like a hedgehog.

Remembering all the mornings he'd had to fight Hadley's profound objections to waking, he tugged the blankets off. "Up and at 'em. C'mon. If you get up now, you can choose your own outfit for school. Otherwise, you're stuck with whatever I pick."

Maddie rolled off the bed and into the pile of plushies. Her tousled head popped up a moment later. She blinked owlishly at him. "I'm up."

"Are you really?" Far too often, his sister had made the same claim and then crawled right back into bed the moment he left the room.

"Can I wear my rainbow tutu to school?"

He didn't see what it would hurt. "Why not? Do you take your lunch to school?"

She nodded, rubbing the sleep from her eyes.

"Okay, I'm gonna go put one together for you. Get dressed and come on into the kitchen. I'm going to make you some breakfast."

"'K."

The *Trolls* lunchbox was on the counter. After starting a pot of coffee, he scoped out the contents of the fridge and pantry and began putting together what he hoped would pass muster for lunch. Classic PB and J sandwich, string cheese, and a little tub of applesauce. Maddie came wandering in as he popped in a strawberry-kiwi juice box to round the whole thing out.

She had, indeed, worn a rainbow tutu, along with purple leggings and, if he wasn't mistaken, at least three shirts, layered one on top of the other.

"You cold?"

"Uh-uh."

"Why so many shirts?"

"I couldn't decide, so I'm wearing them all."

Not up to arguing with that logic, he pointed at the table. "Have a seat."

Instead, she climbed up onto one of the barstools to sit at the counter. "Where's Mommy?"

"Still sleeping. She was extra tired. What do you usually eat for breakfast?"

"Lucky Charms!" The shameless grin told him this was not the truth. Or at least not a weekday truth. Cayla struck him as the sort of mom who might allow a bowl of those on Saturday morning.

"Try again."

Those little shoulders twitched in a shrug. "I don't know."

"Do you like scrambled eggs? Fruit?"

Maddie wrinkled her nose. "Fruit doesn't go in scrambled eggs, silly."

"You're right. It doesn't. You wanna try eggs the way I like them?"

"Okay."

Figuring he could scarf them down if she didn't like them, he pulled out a tomato, onion, bell pepper, cheese, and the carton of eggs and set to dicing.

"How do you like your present?"

Holt glanced over. "My present?"

"Us. Mommy said you needed a family, and that we were gonna play a big game of pretend to give you one."

He went very still. So this was how Cayla had explained things to her. Pretend. He got it. She was protective of her daughter and wouldn't want her getting confused, no matter how genuine the legal ties actually were.

Still, he couldn't quite deny the pinch around his heart at the idea that this wasn't, on some level, real. Which was foolish. He'd known what he was signing on for when he made the offer. This was a marriage of protection. There was friendship and affection between them all. He couldn't expect anything else, no matter how comfortable he'd been in Cayla's bed last night. But he also knew that the only way this ruse would work was if Maddie didn't tell people it was pretend.

"I like it very much. You two are a really special present. But you know what?"

"What?"

"If you tell everybody it's all real, then it'll feel more real. The very best games of pretend are the ones where you forget you're playing. Can you do that?"

"Uh-huh. Can you real-pretend you're my daddy?"

Oh, man, this kid. Holt considered his answer as his heart turned to goo. "Would you like that?"

"I never had a daddy before. And you're fun. Nobody *else's* daddy can do Maui like you."

"Then yeah, if it's okay with you, I'd like to real-pretend that, too."

Maddie beamed. "Okay!" Her smile turned suspicious as he slid a plate of food in front of her. "What's that?"

"Confetti eggs." In truth, it was a lazy man's omelet. Scrambled eggs loaded with veggies and cheese. He knew he was taking a chance putting vegetables in front of a kid her age, when there was a strong possibility she didn't believe in foods touching, but he figured it was worth a try.

He brought his own plate over and sat beside her. "They're my favorite."

She gave the eggs a cautious sniff and shot him a side eye. "Do these have 'gredients?"

"What are 'gredients?"

"Stuff like *broccoli*."

"I can assure you there is no broccoli." He scooped a bite into his mouth. "Mmmm. Cheese. You like cheese, right?"

"Yeah."

"These have cheese. Try 'em. I mean, if you don't want them, I can eat your share." He leaned over, as if to scoop her food onto his plate.

"No! Mine!" She took a hefty, defiant bite. Her little face blanked, and he braced himself for her to spit them back out. "Mmm. I like confetti."

Holt was mentally patting himself on the back when Cayla came rocketing into the room, her hair standing up at all angles, her sleep shirt baring one shoulder. "Oh my God, I overslept!"

Making a concerted effort not to stare at that shoulder, Holt forked up another bite of eggs. "I've got it covered. Have some coffee."

She stared at him, then at her daughter, who'd already almost cleaned her plate, then to the lunchbox ready and waiting at the end of the island, looking for all the world as if someone had struck her upside the head. "You... got her ready for school?"

"Not my first rodeo, and I figured you deserved to sleep in. Yesterday was a lot."

Maddie slid off the stool.

"Go brush your teeth, Bumblebee."

"'K." She skipped her way down the hall, her tutu bouncing.

"And *really* brush them. I'm gonna check!" he called after her.

Cayla's throat worked, unmistakable gratitude shining in her eyes.

It occurred to him that with her ex never having been involved, she'd never had any sort of help other than her mom. She'd never had anyone to pick up the slack or let her sleep in. He vowed he'd do whatever he could to ease some of her burdens while they navigated the threat posed by Raynor. She deserved that.

"I wasn't sure exactly what time she needed to be dropped off or where. You can tell me, and I can take her while you clean up for work, and I'll come back to get you. Or you can grab a quick shower now, and we can both take her and go to work together. I figured it made the most sense for us to stick close together for now."

Crossing the room, she laid a hand on his shoulder. "Thank you. Give me fifteen minutes." Then she leaned in and pressed a soft, lingering kiss to his cheek that had him wishing for so much more of this real-pretend life.

CAYLA NEVER WOULD HAVE IMAGINED the weekday morning routine could be an erotic experience. Then again, she'd never had anyone else's help getting it accomplished. Coming out to find that Holt had wrangled Maddie out of bed, gotten her dressed, fed—with *vegetables*—and otherwise more or less ready for school, all so she herself could sleep in a bit had filled her with so much gratitude that had there been time and an empty house, she quite possibly would have jumped her new husband. Instead, she'd hurried to get dressed and piled in the car with them both for a weirdly domestic ride to school, where Holt and Maddie had sung along to some adult-friendly kid movie playlist he'd found, and she drank her first cup of coffee without having to risk third-degree burns down her throat. If not for the persistent throb between her legs, she'd have been certain she was dreaming again. But surely the dream version of this scenario would have seen her actually following through on her less than PG expression of gratitude.

"What's on your list for today?"

Cayla blinked, dragging her mind away from the start of that fantastic daydream. "I've got a meeting first thing with Misty Pennebaker. She's coming in early, before she opens Moonbeams and Sweet Dreams."

"That's the flower and gift shop downtown, right?"

"Yeah. It's her shop. We work together a lot on events. This happens to be about her upcoming wedding. She was the bride I was out with at karaoke night and is a good friend of mine."

As they neared her little building, Cayla spotted Misty's car out front already. "Oh, no."

Holt tensed. "What is it?"

"What am I going to tell her about us? What are we going to tell *everyone* about us? We weren't even dating, so far as anyone knew, and now we're *married*. People are going to expect a story to go along with that."

He relaxed as he turned into the gravel lot. "Do you trust her with the truth?"

She considered the question. "Yes. She's no gossip. But this is going to keep coming up. We have to have something to tell people about our relationship."

"Then we'll figure it out. Are you free for lunch?"

"Yeah. My other appointments aren't until this afternoon."

"Okay. I'll pop back over then and bring food, and we can get our story straight." Apparently decided, he slid out of the driver's seat.

"Well, okay then," Cayla muttered. She got out herself in time to see Holt wave at a gaping Misty.

He circled around the car and pressed a lingering kiss to her cheek. "I'll see you at lunch. And lock the door." Then he was striding across the street and up the hill to Bad Boy Bakers.

Cayla watched him go, unable to stop herself from admiring the absolute perfection of how he filled out a pair of jeans.

"Girl, what was *that?*" Misty demanded. "You're coming to work in the same car?" She lowered her voice. "Did he spend the night? Did you finally break your sex fast?"

I wish.

On a sigh, Cayla scooped a hand through her hair, trying to figure out what to say.

Misty lunged forward, grabbing her left hand. "Is that...? Are those...? Cayla! Did you two *get married?*"

She blinked down at the rings, thinking it odd that it didn't feel strange to have slid them on this morning. It had been six years since she'd worn wedding rings, and the set she'd been given by Arthur had been massive and ostentatious, so heavy they were almost their own form of mental shackles, reminding her she belonged to him. Her grandmother's rings, slipped on in a judge's chambers by a man she'd known for only a matter of months, felt *right* there. She ran a thumb along the warm circle of gold.

"We, um, kind of eloped yesterday."

Misty squeed so loud that three guys walked out of Willie Thompson's Garage next door to see what the fuss was about. Offering them a little finger waggle, Cayla grabbed her friend by the elbow and towed her inside.

"Oh my God, tell me everything! Don't leave out any details."

"It's not what you think."

"The incredible hunk of hotness that you've been crushing on for months didn't sweep you off your feet?"

"Not exactly."

Picking up on Cayla's less than celebratory mood, she sobered. "You don't seem entirely happy. Was it some kind of crazy drunk mistake?"

"No. No, it was entirely on purpose. I need more coffee for this story." Moving past her to the little kitchenette, Cayla went through the motions of making another pot and admitted what she'd told no one else in town about her ex-husband, before explaining how Arthur was out of prison and that they'd decided to go through with Holt's blurted cover to protect Maddie. "So... yeah, we got married yesterday."

A mug clasped between her palms, coffee all but forgotten, Misty absorbed all of it. "Is that actually going to work?"

"I don't know. I have no idea if it'll be enough to keep Arthur from gaining any sort of custody. I don't know how long it's going to go on or what it's going to do to Maddie when things are over."

"Or what it's going to do to you?" Misty asked gently.

Cayla collapsed back against the counter, wishing she'd already gotten some furniture for this place besides what was in the tiny office in the back. "That's... a consideration."

"How... real is this marriage going to be?"

"I don't know that either. We're both attracted. I'm pretty sure we both have some kind of feelings for each other beyond friendship. But we didn't... well... consummate anything last night. He hasn't even really kissed me." She told Misty what he'd said before bed. "It seems like he's open to more, but he's making sure we don't rush into anything on that front."

"That's a very knight-in-shining-armor-fairy-tale-prince sort of thing to do."

"Yeah," she sighed.

"You don't agree?"

"I do, and I don't. It's sensible. Considerate. But all these feelings are spun up inside me. He's so amazing with Maddie and incredibly thoughtful on so many fronts. Just seeing what needs doing or what might help and doing it without having to be asked. He's like a friggin' unicorn. It would be so very easy to be swept away by that."

"And that's a problem?"

"I've been swept away before, and the prince turned out to be a malignant toad."

"Are you worried Holt will turn out to be something he's not?"

"In the sense that he's somehow a bad guy? No, not at all. A bad guy wouldn't have gone out of his way to do what he's done to protect us. But I can't help worrying and wondering how long it'll be before he starts to feel trapped by his own nobility."

"You think he will?"

"I don't know. Despite the fact that he's attracted, he wasn't going to pursue me before circumstance forced his hand. I don't know if he'll regret this decision, so I'm trying to take things slow and not be swept away by all this forced proximity. No matter how insanely appealing I find him."

"Makes sense. But are you hoping something more real and permanent grows out of this?"

"I wasn't looking for that. It's why I haven't dated since my divorce. But, I mean, you've seen the man. He's smart, funny, sexy as hell, and he adores my daughter. I'd be crazy not to hope this turns into something real." She set her mug aside. "It goes without saying that we won't be sharing the real story with the public, so keep this to yourself."

"Cone of silence, for sure. And I'll do whatever I can to help with things, including slipping the details you want spread into the gossip vine."

That was a thought.

"You just might be onto something. We haven't had time to

figure out what the official story is going to be yet, but obviously there has to be one, and it would be better if we find a way to control the narrative."

"Well, there's one very obvious way to do that."

"And that is?"

Misty's brown eyes twinkled. "Throw a Surprise-We-Eloped! shindig and invite everyone you know."

8

Holt had known Cayla had skills. She'd bootstrapped her event planning business from nothing into a venture that made enough money to support both her and her daughter. But watching her put together a last-minute wedding reception cookout in three days was nothing short of awe-inspiring. It helped that she had an in with basically all the vendors in town. Even the Reynolds sisters, who owned The Misfit Inn and Spa, had been happy to allow her to use the inn as a venue for the party—something they seldom did, he was told.

As the weather was gorgeous, they set up outside, taking advantage of the space normally utilized for the weekly summer Jam Nights the inn hosted for area musicians. Extra string lights had been hung above what constituted the dance floor. Misty had made centerpieces for the mixed assortment of picnic tables, and Cayla had done something with ribbon on chairs, porch rails, and food tables that somehow pulled the look together into a cohesive whole. It all held a relaxed, festive vibe, though most of the attendees didn't know the true purpose of the party. They'd all RSVPed to an e-vite to a show-case for the bakery—again her idea. He figured it was a good sign for their business that nobody had turned it down.

The scent of grilling meat permeated the air. Tables groaned beneath the weight of a myriad of appetizers and desserts. In keeping with the expected theme, he and the guys had provided a big chunk of those. The rest had been subsidized by Athena Reynolds Maxwell, Eden's Ridge's very own award-winning chef. And on a table near the dance floor was the three-tiered chocolate wedding cake he'd slaved over for the past two days. Even though this party was a calculated move to control the story surrounding their marriage, he'd wanted to give Cayla something special from *him*. Cakes were his specialty, and he wanted to wow her.

What he'd done, it seemed, was cast a spell over Maddie. She was circling the table like a shark before a feeding frenzy. When he spotted her little hand reaching for one of the carefully crafted white chocolate roses, he swooped in, scooping her up. "Not so fast. It's not time for cake yet."

Her bottom lip rolled out, her eyes going glassy with crocodile tears. "But you promised you'd make me cake."

"Yep. And you get to have some. Later. But everybody's got to have a chance to see the cake first."

"But there are so many." She dragged the last word out by several syllables of whine. "They'll eat it all!"

"It could be worse, kid. Why don't you go find Mimi?" He set her down, aiming her toward Donna, where she stood across the yard in conversation with someone he hadn't met.

After much discussion, he and Cayla had kept the guest list limited to friends and family, rather than opening the doors to the biggest gossips in town. She had reasoned the news would spread fast enough as it was. Holt was still relatively new in town. Other than his partners, Rebecca, and some of the other

Rangers in the area, he didn't have other friends here yet, so the vast majority of people circulating on the lawn were friends of Cayla's. That was something to see all on its own.

She was so much a part of the fabric of this place. There were so many people, and she had a smile and a kind word for all of them. She was every bit as much of a bumblebee as her daughter, moving from cluster to cluster, spreading her sunshine. He couldn't help but be a little in awe of that. That sort of connection didn't come easy for him. It certainly wasn't how he'd grown up.

A hand slid through the crook of his arm. "I spy, with my little eye, a man who can't take his eyes off his woman."

Holt glanced down at Rebecca, his surrogate mom since he'd moved to Eden's Ridge. "You know what's going on." He'd given her the update himself as she'd cut his hair just before the wedding.

"That doesn't make it any less true. You two look good together."

Because he liked the sound of that way too much, he grunted. "We're pulling things off."

She squeezed his arm. "Enjoy tonight, Holt. Regardless of circumstances, it's for the two of you."

Before he could form a retort, she looked off toward the dance floor, where Jonah was taking a microphone from Flynn Bohannon, one of the Reynolds sisters' husbands. "Looks like it's about time for things to get started."

A muffled thump came over the sound system. "Is this thing on? Oh, there it is. Hey everybody! I'm Jonah Ferguson, and on behalf of Bad Boy Bakers, I'd like to thank all y'all for coming out tonight."

In accordance with the plan, Holt and Brax began moving toward the stage to join him as applause rippled through the crowd.

"I'd like to introduce my business partners, Brax Whitmore and Holt Steele. They'd like to say a little something."

Brax took the mic. "I'm Brax. As Jonah said, thank you for coming out tonight. And thank you for all the early support you've shown our bakery. We look forward to a big turnout at our grand opening in a couple of weeks."

He passed the mic to Holt, who had to swallow before speaking. "Hi. It's great to see everybody here, and I hope you enjoy the sampling of our food and the party that Cayla worked so hard to put together. Cayla, why don't you come on up here and take a well-deserved bow?"

She joined them under the cafe lights, beaming a smile as she made a curtsy and took the mic from him. "Thank you, gentlemen. And thank all of y'all for coming out tonight to support Bad Boy Bakers." She waited for the applause to die down before continuing to speak. "Now, here's the part where we make our confession: This party isn't actually about the bakery, although they did absolutely supply the lion's share of the food."

A murmur ran through the assembly as everybody looked at each other, trying to figure out what was really going on.

"See, the thing about being an event planner is that you're usually so busy planning everyone else's special occasions that you don't have time to plan your own, and you kinda squeeze things in as you can." With a smile, she held her hand out, and Holt took it. "Like spontaneously eloping on a Tuesday. This is actually our Surprise! We're married! reception."

There were hoots and hollers and a few "Holy shit!"s.

Cayla laughed, and the sound was its own music, not coming off the least bit staged. "I know this comes as a *tremendous* surprise since we basically didn't tell anyone we were dating. But, well, when you know, you know."

Her eyes met his, and all Holt could think was, *Yeah.*

"—so we pulled the trigger."

He knew that this speech was largely performative. She was setting the stage, getting the word out. But he couldn't resist pulling her back against him, tucking his head over her shoulder to press a kiss to the strip of skin along her collarbone. She trembled a little, her hand rising to comb through his hair. The microphone caught her little sigh.

Somebody let out a wolf whistle.

Cayla cleared her throat. "Right, so, we wanted to invite all of you here tonight to celebrate, have some cake and some dancing, and share in our mutual joy. Thank you for coming!"

She tossed the microphone without even looking and spun into him.

A laughing Jonah apparently caught it. "Congratulations, you two! How about we have the first dance?"

Cayla's fingers dug into his shoulder as she looked up at him with unmistakable heat. Though he'd shared her bed every night after the first, he hadn't pushed for more. She'd been manipulated in horrible fashion by her ex, and he didn't want to do the same, no matter how much he wanted her. But he was grateful for the excuse to hold her close now. Thrilled to have reason to keep his hands on her.

"So Cayla's daughter Maddie helped with the playlists for tonight, and she was *very* particular about what the first dance song should be."

"Did you know anything about this part?" Cayla asked.

"No."

When the steel drums sounded over the PA, followed by the smooth high strings, they both laughed, and he nudged her into a gentle sway. "'Kiss The Girl'. Of course."

Cayla's eyes sparkled. "Didn't know you'd be doing the first dance serenaded by a Disney crab, did you?"

He grinned. "I think we're being match-made by the five-year-old."

"That does appear to be the case." Her pupils sprang wide, even as much of the crowd picked up the song and began to sing along. "So, are we gonna give the people what they want?"

It was his turn to swallow. He knew the cursory cheek kisses weren't going to sell this. But he didn't want to sell it. He wanted to live it. He wanted his wife to want him. "I'm a whole lot more concerned with giving you what you want."

Her cheeks flushed and her voice went husky as she whispered, "Then kiss me."

He was giving that kid the biggest slice of chocolate cake ever.

Lowering his head, he took her mouth, intending to only have a taste. Something appropriate for the audience that wouldn't do more than draw out an awww or raise a brow or two. But Cayla opened for him, softening and blooming against him until the flavor of her soaked into his blood and set him on fire. He was absolutely lost. But also found. She was everything he'd hoped and so much more. He needed an island with total privacy for at least a decade or so to slake this devastating need she roused.

The dim, distant sound of whooping and cheering reminded him they were most definitely not on a desert island. And the song was evidently long over. With the reluctance of waking from the best dream, he lifted his head.

Cayla's cheeks were gorgeously flushed, her lips red and swollen from his, her eyes glazed with lust. "We have to actually stick around for the party, don't we?"

"Probably."

"Damn," she whispered.

Holt grinned and held her close. "We've got time. I'm not going anywhere."

Her arms tightened around him. "Good."

And as they braced themselves to face their guests, he

hoped like hell that this was actually the start of something instead of more of their game of real-pretend.

LETTING Maddie have two pieces of cake had been a terrible idea. Not that Holt had given her permission, nor had he actually seen it happen, but given the fact that it was a solid two hours past her bedtime and she was still doing the little girl version of zoomies around the house, he was pretty sure it was a reasonable assumption.

"Surely, she'll crash soon," he murmured.

Cayla's gaze followed her daughter's flight. "This is one of those moments when I consider the acceptability of sedating her with Benadryl."

"No jury of your peers would convict you." Especially not as they'd both been desperate to get through the party to follow up on all the wants generated by that kiss.

"Probably not. But we're going to try a few other things first. How are you with wrestling?"

Holt shot her a look. "I'm guessing you're not talking about the naked variety?"

Her brown eyes met his, full of heat. "Not yet."

There is a God.

"See if you can work off some of her energy while I draw a bath. She's going to smell like a lavender farm when she's out."

Rolling his shoulders, he fixed his eyes on his pint-sized target. "On it."

Holt scooped Maddie up and took her down to the floor in a smooth roll, letting her crawl all over him before tickling her ribs until she shrieked with laughter.

"Surrender, tiny human!"

"Never!" Her little fingers found their way to his own ticklish spots, digging in until he was wriggling and laughing himself.

"Bath time, children."

At the sound of her mother's voice, Maddie looked up and Holt took advantage, flipping her over to blow a raspberry on her belly. She flailed, narrowly missing his kidney as she giggled with hysterics.

"Say Uncle!"

"But I don't have an uncle."

Holt paused. "That's a fair point."

Cayla held out her hand. "C'mon, Munchkin."

Maddie scrambled up and followed Cayla into the bathroom. Bath time took another twenty minutes, then the little lavender-scented schemer bartered for two more chapters of *Mr. Popper's Penguins*. But apparently that was enough because her eyes drooped closed before they got halfway through the second. Cayla eyed her carefully as she read another couple of paragraphs, but Maddie didn't move. They both eased off the bed, making their silent escape.

By tacit agreement, they began picking up the disaster left by Hurricane Maddie. In the quiet, Holt heard the patter of rain against the front windows. "Glad that held off until the party was over."

"Yeah, moving things indoors would've been a pain. But I think the reception went really well."

He finished tossing the last of Maddie's stuffed animals into the basket and turned to watch Cayla finish tidying up the couch cushions, the shape of her backside a tantalizing curve in that pretty dress.

"Seems like it definitely did what it was supposed to do. I've lived here long enough to recognize that everyone in town will know we're married by Monday morning."

He was a whole lot more concerned with *feeling* very

married after tonight. But he wouldn't push her here. She was calling the shots.

Straightening, Cayla strode over to him, sliding her arms up his chest to link behind his neck. "It did a few other things, too."

And just like that, his body was ready to go. Zero to Reporting-For-Duty-Sir in less than ten syllables. Judging by the darkening of Cayla's eyes, his wife was very aware of it, too. With one of those secret, female smiles, she took his hand and pulled him into their bedroom. Because somehow, in the past few days, it had become theirs, not just hers.

Very deliberately, she locked the door behind them. And this wasn't at all like that first night. There was no hesitation. No avoidance of eye contact. Her intent was clear, but he needed to hear her say it.

"Are you sure?"

Her hands stroked up his pecs. "Absolutely."

"Thank God." He reached for her, his hands curving around her hips, circling her into another dance.

She laughed. "What would you have done if I'd said no?"

"Backed off. And probably cried."

She was grinning as she brought her mouth back to brush his. "No crying tonight."

"Only the good kind," he promised. Because he needed to hear more of those little sighs she'd let out earlier.

Cayla shuddered and moaned a little, her fingers working at the buttons of his shirt as they circled toward the bed. Holt loved the feel of her hands on him as she tugged the shirt free and pushed it off his shoulders. He pulled off his undershirt himself and enjoyed the hell out of the appreciative gaze she raked over his chest. Her fingers followed, tracing each ridge of muscle. Damn, that felt good.

Because he needed more, he reached for the row of tiny buttons that ran down the front of her dress. He fumbled on the first half dozen, his fingers feeling about as adept as sausages.

"Did you pick this dress to torture me?"

Her low laugh was throaty. "No, that's just a side benefit."

Holt had no doubt that she could undo them faster than he could. But she didn't offer, instead standing patiently, seeming to enjoy the anticipation as he slowly exposed each new inch of her, until the dress gaped open down to her waist, showing a flash of pink lace. On an inhale, he nudged the dress off her shoulders, watching as it slithered down to the floor, leaving her in only a matching set of bra and panties.

He let out a reverent curse. "You're beautiful."

She stepped into him again, her hands going to his belt. "And yours."

A roll of thunder seemed to underscore the point.

Hell, yes.

Taking her mouth in a deep, drugging kiss, he wrapped around her, his fingers working at the clasp of her bra.

The bedroom door flew open, banging back against the wall. He didn't think, just spun, automatically putting himself between Cayla and the threat, his hands raised.

Maddie rocketed across the room, taking a flying leap onto the bed as another, bigger crash of thunder sounded. She whimpered and dove under the covers.

Cayla sucked in a shuddering breath and dropped her brow to his shoulder. "She's afraid of thunderstorms."

"Ah." It was all he could manage with all the blood drained out of his head.

He was still staring at the open door—the one they'd locked —when she stepped away to snag her sleep shirt off the chair. She slipped it on, doing some kind of female contortion to take the bra off from underneath.

With a look of apology, she climbed into bed to check on the shivering lump under the covers, and Holt understood that their delayed wedding night had just been put on the back burner. Again.

"Hey, Bumblebee, it's time."

Cayla's hand shot out to grab the sippy cup that flew off the coffee table as Maddie scrambled up from the picture she was coloring and made a beeline for the front door.

Holt scooped her up with one arm. "Hold it. Shoes."

Maddie kicked her feet as if running in place from where he held her off the floor. He leaned over to grab the slip-ons off the rack by the door and dropped them down, lowering her until she could slide her feet in. Then he opened the door, letting her dangle for a bit as Cayla came to join them. She could see Maddie's quarry by the curb.

Her feet churned like the Roadrunner. "Lemme down! Lemme down!"

God, Cayla loved her kid. Unable to contain the smile, she looked over at Holt. His blue eyes sparkled, the corners of his mouth turned up in the barest of smiles. It was a potent thing, being able to share her joy in Maddie with someone else. She hadn't realized how much she'd wanted that. How much pleasure she'd get seeing someone else's appreciation for the unique little human she was raising.

On her nod, Holt let Maddie loose.

"Leno!"

Cayla smiled as Maddie raced down the front sidewalk to where Mia and Brax waited with their massive pit bull for the official evening love fest. Leno dipped low in a play bow, his entire butt wiggling as she approached. They collided with mutual joy on both sides, as they did almost every night.

Holt slid an arm around Cayla's waist as they followed Maddie out of the house. "That kid needs a dog."

She mirrored the gesture, enjoying the brush of his body against hers, reveling in the awareness of his warmth and the touch she certainly hadn't gotten enough of. "That kid *wants* a dog. I do not have the bandwidth to add another creature to take care of to this household. Not right now. She's happy loving on Leno." And if the sounds of absolute delight from her daughter gave her a little pinch of guilt over that fact, well, it was a pinch she'd learned to ignore. She had to be practical.

They strolled down to the street, his big hand possessively curved around her hip in a way that had her thinking about far fewer clothes and no audience. Dragging her mind away from the honeymoon that hadn't yet been, she called out, "Evening, y'all."

"Guess what!" Maddie demanded.

They all dutifully chorused, "What?"

"Today at school, Mary Beth told everybody about how her dog Rocket ate her glow in the dark crayons."

"Uh-oh. I bet that upset his tummy," Mia observed.

"I don't know about that, but she said he's been having glow in the dark poops!"

Holt snickered. "Well, then I guess they know where to scoop."

Maddie nodded soberly. "Responsibible dog owners scoop the poop."

"They do," Brax agreed."

"Know what else they do?"

"What's that?" he asked.

"They make sure their puppers have other doggie friends to play with."

"Socialization is important," Mia said.

Maddie turned guileless eyes on Cayla. "See? Socialzition is portnant. We should get a friend to help do that for Leno."

Always an operator, her child. "Nice try, Munchkin."

She shrugged with an unrepentant grin. "Can't blame a girl for tryin'."

"Bath time, Little Miss. Say goodnight to Leno and Mia and Brax."

"Goodnight, Leno. You're the bestest boy ever." Maddie dropped a kiss to his enormous head.

Leno barked in agreement.

"Night Mia! Night Brax!"

"Night, Maddie. See you later." Mia lifted her hand in a wave as the two of them moved on to continue their walk.

Cayla waved in return and began herding her offspring back toward the house. "Holt, can you check the mail?"

"Sure thing."

It took longer than she wanted to get her chattering daughter settled in the bath, bribed with pink bubbles. There were still dinner dishes to wash, and she really ought to get a load of laundry on, so she could swap it over to the dryer before bed. Mind full of everything still to do, she wandered into the kitchen, already rolling up her sleeves.

Holt intercepted her before she could get to the sink. "Dishes can wait a minute."

"Oh, but I really need to—"

"They can wait," he insisted, stabbing a few buttons on his phone, until music spilled out of the little bluetooth speaker she kept on the counter. Ed Sheeran.

"What are you up to?"

He tugged her into his arms and circled her to the beat. "Dancing with you. It's become one of my favorite things."

She relaxed against him, enjoying the sway of his body against hers. "Mmm. I'm pretty fond of it myself." And of all the memories dancing evoked of that panty-melting kiss they'd shared at their reception. They still hadn't moved beyond those kisses. Much as Maddie seemed intent on matchmaking them, she wanted to be there to encourage the connection, so there hadn't been an opportunity for more than a handful of stolen kisses and heated glances during the days. Add to that multiple nights running of them ending up with a squirming child in their bed courtesy of a series of thunderstorms in the area, and nights had been out, too. She and her daughter needed to have a conversation about how she and Holt weren't like her dolls, and they needed uninterrupted time to themselves. But Cayla hadn't figured out how to brave that discussion.

As Holt's big, broad palm pressed against her lower back, she found she was enjoying where they were, lingering in this long, drawn out seduction. Anticipation heightened each new touch and sensation. At this point, there was no questioning, no second guessing. Whatever else they felt, however long this lasted, right now they wanted each other, and that was a heady delight. No doubt, they could've gotten creative and carved out time for a quickie, but neither of them wanted to rush. Unfortunately, her calendar of appointments and events had been utterly packed even before they'd gotten married. Holt's workdays were getting busier and busier, as he and the guys prepared for the official grand opening of Bad Boy Bakers. So she'd take this little slice of domestic romance and be grateful.

Resting her head against his shoulder, she sighed. "I could totally get used to dancing in the kitchen after dinner."

"Doesn't get much better than this," he agreed.

"Oh, I don't know about that." Lifting her head, she rose up, finding his mouth for another of those toe-curling kisses she was getting addicted to.

Holt groaned low in his throat, his arms tightening around her. She loved feeling the flex of his muscles against her and couldn't wait for the chance to touch and explore every bare inch of him. He was so strong and capable, beautifully made, all the way down to the scars she'd glimpsed but hadn't asked about. She'd never wanted like this. Never craved someone else's touch this much. And if she didn't have his hands on every bare inch of her soon, she just might go insane.

"Mommy! I'm done!" As Maddie's bellow echoed down the hall, Holt broke the kiss.

Cayla whimpered. "We could duct tape her to the wall, maybe. Just for an hour or two."

"I don't think even duct tape can hold up to her energy. Maybe she'll stay in her own bed tonight."

"I think you're becoming her new favorite stuffed animal. I'm getting jealous."

A laugh rumbled in his chest. "Parents across the world have more than one kid, so clearly they're figuring this out somehow."

"Hardware store. There has to be a lock for the door that won't just pop open on a sneeze."

"We'll look into it." With another quick kiss, he let her go. "You want dishes or jammies?"

"Dishes. She argues less with you about bed. I'm riding the novelty of that as long as it lasts."

"Okay. I'll get her pajamafied."

Alone again, Cayla blew out a breath. Feeling restless and needy, she threw herself into doing the dishes, loading plates and bowls into the dishwasher and scrubbing up pots and pans. From the bathroom she could hear the two of them belting out "We Don't Talk About Bruno". She laughed to herself, marveling at how easily Holt had slid into their everyday lives, becoming a part of long-established routines. No matter how he'd gotten here, he fit with their family. It was a backward way to build a relationship, but it *did* feel as if they were building one. That made this easier.

Still smiling at the impromptu concert, she picked up the stack of mail he'd brought in and riffled through it. A letter with a return address to a bank she didn't have an account with had her pausing. Slipping a finger beneath the flap, she ripped the envelope open. All her simple pleasure in the evening evaporated she skimmed the contents.

Someone had tried to open a credit card account using her information. The application had failed because her credit reports were locked.

And so it begins.

She knew things had been oddly quiet since Arthur's threat. Here was the confirmation that he hadn't miraculously given up his claim. And it was a good reminder not to get too comfortable in this little Twilight Zone life she'd landed in. They were both making the best of a strange situation. But the bloom would fade, probably sooner rather than later, and then where would they be? How long would it take Holt's regrets to fester?

He trotted in, a giggling Maddie on his back in her Paw Patrol pajamas. He took one look at her face and sobered. "What is it?"

"Nothing that can't wait until after bed. I believe we owe someone another chapter of *Mr. Popper's Penguins.*"

"Yeah!"

Somehow, Cayla put the letter out of her head for the duration of the bedtime routine, losing herself in the story and snuggles from her little girl. She finished the chapter, and Maddie begged for one more song from Holt. Then they kissed her goodnight and left her guarded by her menagerie.

Holt said nothing until they reached the kitchen. "Raynor's done something."

"He's tried." She poured herself a half glass of wine and sat at the table, nudging the letter toward him. "I should have expected he'd pull something like this. It makes sense that he'd strike out in habitual ways. I expected it when I left him, so I locked down my credit reports and Maddie's. I should have thought of this before. If yours aren't locked, they need to be, immediately."

"How would he have gotten my information? He doesn't even have my name."

"I have no idea. But identity theft is what he does, remember? And as far as he's concerned, you're now enemy number one, so I promise he can find it out. We shouldn't take the risk."

"Okay. I'll take care of it." He pulled her into his lap, rubbing at the knots that had formed in her shoulders. "We knew he'd do something. As an opening volley, this isn't that bad. No harm actually done. And nothing to do with custody of Maddie."

She slid her arms around his shoulders, soaking in his solid, steady strength. "That's what worries me. He won't be satisfied with this. It's too small. Too simple. This is... like kicking tires. Like he's trying to find the chink in our defenses. Or distract us from seeing something else."

"You're smart. Careful. We'll find any holes and shore them up. It's gonna be okay. If and when he takes legal action, we'll be ready for him."

She bit her lip, wondering if that was actually true. "It's so hard to predict what he'll do. In some senses, I know him. But I don't understand him. I don't understand people like him, who would rather profit off others than put in the work to build something real. How he thinks doesn't make sense to me, and I don't want to end up blindsided because of it."

"Could you reach out to your FBI contact? The one you dealt with to put him away in the first place?"

"I should. I don't know if there's anything he can tell me about the retrial, but it's worth letting him know that there's a strong possibility that Arthur is up to his old tricks again."

"Even if he can't tell you, he might be able to tell Xander as sheriff. We should update him on the situation. There still may be nothing that's grounds for a restraining order, but keeping local law enforcement in the loop isn't a bad idea. It's one more person on your side."

Threading her fingers in the hair at the base of his neck, she searched his face. "I'm glad you're on my side. That you're in my life." As he leaned into the touch, his eyes falling to half mast, she decided to be honest. "I admit, I'm a little afraid of you."

His eyes snapped open, his hands going still. "You are?"

"Not like that." It was her turn to rub at the new knots in his shoulders. "It's just... you've integrated so thoroughly into our lives in less than two weeks. It's been so easy with you, and I learned a long time ago not to trust easy. I think you'd have done whatever was necessary to smooth that transition because that's the mission, and I have no doubt that you were very, *very* good at what you did before. Don't get me wrong. I'm enjoying this bizarre backwards dating thing we've been doing. But I can't help but wonder what happens when the mission is over? When—God willing—Arthur goes back to prison."

She could see him weighing his words, and her gut tightened with anxiety over what they might be.

"You're not wrong. I lived a mission-centered life for a long, long time. And maybe there's some of that in how I've approached things because it's just how I've been trained. But you're more than a mission for me. I'm not going through all of this with some eye toward the exit date. Maybe I wouldn't have pursued things with you without some external push, but that was only because I think you deserve better."

Cayla frowned. "Better than what?"

"Me."

Horrified and furious in equal measure, she cupped his face between her palms. "Why would you say that? I don't care what you may have come from growing up. I don't care what you may have done as part of your service. I don't care that it took a piece of you—not beyond the fact that it had to have hurt you tremendously. You're kind and generous, fiercely loyal, with the biggest heart you don't seem to want anyone to know about. Those are the measure of a man, and you're the best one I know. So don't you dare insult the man I married by somehow suggesting he's less."

His throat worked.

Cayla couldn't stop herself from skimming her thumbs along his cheeks. She softened her voice. "Are we clear?"

"Yes, ma'am."

She lowered her mouth to his for a soft, quiet kiss that soothed them both. Whatever other issues they had to face, she was determined that him feeling worthy wouldn't be one of them.

9

"**A**re you *sure* you don't mind this? I know you have a ton to do to get ready for the grand opening."

Holt waited until Cayla had fastened her earrings before turning her from the bathroom mirror to face him and boxing her in against the counter, one arm planted on either side of her hips. "I've got this. Maddie and I will be fine. And I swear I'll make sure she eats something that isn't pure sugar."

Her chest rose and fell in a heavy sigh as her hands skated up his chest and over his shoulders to toy with the hair at his nape. "I'm not questioning your capability. I just... don't want to take advantage."

Wanting to purr at her touch, he lowered his mouth to a hair's breadth from hers. "You can take advantage of me anytime."

Cayla groaned. "I'd like the chance to take that kind of advantage of you at all. And I know we could probably squeeze in something fast under current circumstances, but as this past week has shown, the likelihood of getting interrupted is high, and as hard as this is, being interrupted further along in the... uh... process just seems mean."

A laugh rumbled up in his chest. "You're not wrong. And I suppose there's something to be said for anticipation."

Her smile was wry. "If my anticipation dials up much more, all you're going to have to do is look at me."

"There's something to aspire to." Easing back, he dragged his gaze from her face down to her chest, imagining the sight of those lovely full breasts without the restriction of bra and dress. Her nipples pebbled as he watched, and he grinned.

"There's going to be no living with you now, is there?"

"Don't worry. I understand that with great power comes great responsibility." To illustrate the point, he gripped her by the hips and sat her on the counter.

"What are you doing?" Cayla's voice was gratifyingly breathless and her knees automatically parted to accommodate him.

"The way I see it is this: Yeah, we'd both like a big chunk of uninterrupted time to explore each other. But at this point, we're probably more distracted from the things we're supposed to be doing by thinking about getting naked together. So it seems prudent to take the edge off." He skimmed his palms up her torso.

"But Maddie—ooooh." Her voice trailed off on a moan as he cupped her breasts over the dress, circling those pert nipples with his thumbs.

"She's currently enraptured by old episodes of *Voltron*. On the other side of the bedroom door, which is locked, with the chair in front. You don't have to be out the door for fifteen more minutes, and under the circumstances, I don't think you're going to take that long."

Those brown eyes were glazed with lust as she smiled. "Cocky, aren't you?"

"It's not cocky when it's justified. I need to get my hands on you. Need to taste you. Just a little to get me through. Please?"

"Well, what kind of wife would I be if I said no to such a polite request?"

Oh, hell yeah. He loved the sound of that.

Dipping his hand into the neckline of her dress, he freed one beautiful breast, immediately bending to take that pearled nipple into his mouth. Cayla's breath exploded out, her fingers threading into his hair. She was so damned sweet, so responsive to each swirl and pull of his tongue. Judging by those little whimpering cries she was trying to muffle, he could probably make her come just from this. But he wanted to give her more. Because she'd given him back a piece of himself he hadn't even known was missing, and he knew he was a drowning man slipping under for the third time.

Switching over to the other breast, he stroked his free hand up her leg, beneath the skirt of her dress, to the heated juncture between her thighs. She immediately rocked into his touch, and he felt the dampness of her underwear. Shifting them aside, he cupped her, growling as he parted her folds and felt all that hot, slick wetness against his palm. For him.

It took all his control not to lose it right then and there. But he'd made her a promise, and he intended to deliver.

One finger breached that waiting heat, and she cried out. Abandoning her breast, he took her mouth, swallowing her moans of pleasure, as he slid a second finger into that tight channel, imagining it was his dick she was riding with abandon. He wanted her over him, so he could watch those gorgeous breasts bounce as he thrust inside her. He'd gone so hard behind his fly, the zipper was probably leaving a permanent imprint. But it was absolutely worth it for every buck, every sound, every taste of her passion. This was his *wife*. His. And on that absolutely caveman thought, he dragged his thumb through her wetness and circled her clit.

She exploded, her inner muscles clamping down, her whole body bowing into him. The aftershocks seemed to go on and on, until at last she lay limp and trembling against his shoulder, breath heaving.

"You are... that was... We're going to need a defibrillator for the bedroom. If you can do that with your hands and mouth, actually having you inside me may give me a heart attack."

Despite the total lack of blood supply to his brain, Holt kissed her with smug satisfaction. "Four minutes."

Cayla made an incoherent noise he eventually identified as a laugh. "Your master plan failed, though."

"You don't feel better?"

"I feel amazing. But if you think I'm not going to be thinking about getting you naked even more now, you're sorely mistaken."

He grinned. "Worth it."

"Let me up. I need to clean up before I leave."

"Just one second." Reaching beneath her dress, he dragged her panties down and off. "I'm keeping these."

The fire engine blush on her cheeks when he stuffed them in his pocket was something else that was going to stick with him for the rest of the day.

Holt got his raging hard on under control by the time Cayla had made herself presentable again. Maddie was still glued to *Voltron.*

"I'm gonna be gone all day for work. You be good for Holt. Okay, baby?"

"Uh huh."

"Madeleine Faith, I'm speaking to you."

Maddie dragged her gaze from the TV. "Sorry, Mommy. Have a good day!"

"I probably won't be back until after dinner. Hugs."

As soon as Maddie was done squeezing her, Holt stepped up for his turn. "I'll get by the hardware store sometime today."

"See that you do." She framed his face and gave him a lingering kiss. "Incentive."

"Yes, ma'am."

Then she was gone, and he was alone with his pint-sized charge.

"Okay, Bumblebee, time to get dressed. We're gonna be at the bakery today."

"Does that mean I get cake?"

"You'll have to work for it. I need an assistant baker to help me with recipes today. You up for it?"

"Yeah!" Lured by the prospect of chocolate, she abandoned *Voltron* and raced for her room.

Brax and Jonah were already at Bad Boy Bakers by the time they arrived. Given the bowls, trays, and other baking implements scattered over work surfaces, they had been for a while.

"Good mornin', Sunshine," Jonah announced. "Hi to you, too, Holt."

Maddie giggled. "Hi! Whatcha makin'?"

"Cat head biscuits."

Her eyes went huge and horrified. "You're cooking kitty cats?"

"No! No. They're really big biscuits. The size of a kitty cat's head. No kitties were harmed in the making of this breakfast. Cross my heart." Jonah made an X over his chest and lifted her up so she could see the biscuits baking in one of their industrial ovens.

"The cat head biscuits are delicious but I keep telling him the butter dip tray biscuits are more practical for breakfast sandwiches," Brax argued. "We can prep the whole thing at once. Less effort, equally delicious. We're a bakery. We don't want to have to make the fillings fresh for every order."

"Yeah, but the cat heads can be made in smaller batches. Until we know what kind of traffic we're looking at, we don't want to waste ingredients by overcooking."

These had become familiar debates as they neared their

grand opening. Holt stowed his keys and walked over to his workstation. "What do the numbers say?"

As they talked, Maddie wandered the kitchen, little hands clasped behind her back to keep herself from touching anything. Holt kept half an eye out to make sure she didn't try to touch the ovens or range while he began gathering ingredients from the storeroom and walk-in cooler. He figured he could make up some fondant for her to use like Play-doh.

"What's back here?"

"That's the office," Brax explained.

She tugged open the door and peered into the tiny room. "Looks like a closet to me."

"That's because it was totally a closet," Holt told her. "We didn't think about needing office space when we did the renovation, so we kinda had to shoe-horn one in where we could." They'd fashioned a desk out of a pair of file cabinets with some boards laid over the top. A desktop computer—one of his friend Cash's cast-offs from his cybersecurity business—sat on top. Shelves of the same iron pipe and pallet board they'd used out front filled the wall above it. It wasn't anything to write home about, but it was a functional workspace for doing inventory or accounting.

"What about this one?"

"That door goes outside. Technically, it's our delivery entrance. Mostly, it's where we go to take out the trash. Which needs doing now." Holt raised a brow at his partners as he grabbed the bag from the communal can and twisted it closed. "Open the door for me, will you, kiddo?"

She twisted the knob, pushing the door open and holding it for him.

"Thanks." He strode past her, the bag of trash held high.

Something crashed, and one of the garbage cans fell over. Holt turned to see a skinny little dog scarfing down banana peels from the bag it had torn open. What kind of hungry did a dog have to be to eat *banana* peels?

From behind him, Maddie squeaked and leapt forward. His heart clawed its way into his throat as he lunged for her and missed. She was going to get bitten. Hurt. On his watch. The dog reared up, and he braced to dive between snapping jaws and the child.

She was... giggling.

The dog had its front paws on her shoulders and was bathing her face with its tongue. Maddie had her arms around it, grinning in absolute delight.

Holt's knees went weak with relief, and he had to reach out and steady himself against the wall of the building. The dog was friendly. Walking over, he gently lifted it off Maddie's shoulders. It immediately flopped onto its back. Her back, he noted, as she wriggled in obvious demand for belly scratches, the skinny whip of a tail swishing against the ground.

He couldn't quite stop himself from complying. "What are we gonna do about you?"

"Well, that's easy, silly. She's hungry. We should feed her."

"Feed who?" Jonah stuck his head out the door. "Oh."

Brax followed him out. "I see we have a guest."

"Yeah, she could do with something more appropriate to eat than banana peels. But we've got to figure out who she belongs to." Even as Holt said it, he knew this dog didn't belong to anybody. She wore no collar and was far too skinny—maybe forty pounds when she should've been over fifty—with each of her ribs showing against the dirty brown coat. She'd clearly been on her own for a significant amount of time.

The dog rolled back to her feet, whole body vibrating from wags as she leaned against Maddie. Maddie draped one arm over her shoulders, and they both looked up at him with pleading eyes.

Gah. Those eyes! He'd been trained to withstand all manner of torture, but this. This was just fighting dirty.

Needing some kind of backup, Holt looked at his friends.

Brax just grinned. "Brother, you're screwed."

It was a good day that started with an orgasm and ended with ecstatic clients and multiple referrals. Cayla decided bookending that day with another orgasm—preferably a mutual one this time—would make it even better. She wondered if Holt had made it to the hardware store, and if he'd had a chance to install the new lock yet. Hope sprang eternal.

He hadn't contacted her today other than to say he'd have dinner on warm for when she got home. She could only hope that was because all had been calm and quiet, with nothing new from Arthur and no major misbehavior on Maddie's part. She was a good kid, but this was the first day she'd been with Holt entirely on their own. Undoubtedly, she'd be testing his boundaries as a parental figure. Cayla just hoped it hadn't been too trying for him.

She stepped into the kitchen to the smell of onions, peppers, and tomatoes, with a heavy hint of garlic. Spaghetti, if her nose didn't deceive her. Her mouth watered, anticipating a plateful, hopefully with a slice of rich, buttery garlic bread.

Holt appeared in the doorway from the living room. "You're home."

"I am." Feeling buoyant and happy, she skipped across the room, much as her daughter tended to, and bounced up to kiss him soundly on the mouth. "I had the best day."

"Good! The wedding went well?"

"It went absolutely fantastic. And I ended up with *four* referrals by the end of the reception."

"That's worth drinking to. Let me pour you a glass of wine."

"I won't say no." She wandered over to grab a plate and began filling it from the pots on the stove as she gave him the high points of the day.

It wasn't until she reached for the wine that she took a close look at his face. He looked... guilty. Not quite meeting her eyes as he handed her the glass.

Her own smile faded. "What is it?"

He fidgeted, a move so uncharacteristic she knew something was definitely wrong.

"Holt? Did something happen? Did Arthur show up?"

His hand shot out to cover hers and squeezed. "No. No, nothing like that."

She realized she had yet to see or hear any sign of her daughter and felt fresh panic begin to brew. "Where's Maddie?"

"She's absolutely fine. Don't worry. She's playing out back."

That was when Cayla heard the barking. On a narrow-eyed glare, she strode to the window and saw Maddie romping around the yard with an unfamiliar dog.

She rounded on him. "Holt! You can't just get her a dog without discussing it with me. I expressly told you the other day that I couldn't handle adding another living thing to this household. How could you do this?"

"I know. And I didn't. I mean, not on purpose. I swear, it's not my fault! She pulled a *Puss In Boots.*"

"What are you talking about?"

He scrubbed a hand over his head. "We were at the bakery, and I took the trash out, and Maddie came out with me, and there was this dog digging through the garbage. We couldn't just leave her there. She was clearly starving. But when I told Maddie we had to find out who she belonged to, she looked at me with these *eyes.* Like I was the worst person in the world if I didn't bring her home with us. I've survived waterboarding, sensory deprivation, and a whole host of other things I'd never describe to you, and I couldn't say no to a five-year-old."

Cayla didn't want a dog. She didn't have the bandwidth for a dog. But she knew exactly what face he was talking about, and she recognized she probably should've warned him about it.

"Rookie move, Steele. Parenting 101 means you are required to withstand the utilization of The Face. Otherwise, total chaos reigns and you end up raising little tyrants."

"I know. And I get it. But look at them, Cayla. Are you really going to be the one to take that away from her?"

He turned her toward the window again so she could see Maddie flopping on the grass with her new four-legged companion in the fading light, the world's biggest smile on her face as the dog cuddled into her. They were close enough Cayla could count the poor animal's ribs. If she'd had a home, it wasn't a good one. And the county animal shelter was already under-funded and over-crowded. She was a bleeding heart. The only way she'd been able to say no this long was that no situation like this had presented itself. But she could no more put that dog in a kill shelter or kick her out on the street than she could let go of her own child.

"I kind of hate you a little bit right now."

"Fair. Would it help if I promised to do all the cleaning up after the dog and teaching Maddie how to be responsible for her?"

"It's a start."

She tried to hold herself stiff as he tugged her back against his body, wrapping those strong arms around her as he bent his mouth close to her ear. "How about if I promise to make up for the inconvenience and additional stress with baked goods and orgasms?"

Her lips twitched. "I suppose that depends."

"On what?"

"Did you actually make it to the hardware store today?"

His silence was answer enough.

Cayla sighed and pulled away.

"I really meant to. But once Banana Bread turned up, we got kinda busy, going down to the co-op to buy dog food and a bed and a crate and supplies, and then getting her home and bathed and settled and... Yeah. By the time I thought of it again, they were already closed."

"Banana Bread?"

"She was eating banana peels from the trash when we found her, so that's what Maddie named her. I was thinking we could call her BB for short."

In that moment he looked so young himself, with a boyish hope shining in those big blue eyes.

"Did you have a dog growing up?"

He blinked, some shutter going down over the hope. "No. We lived in an apartment. It wasn't practical."

God. She couldn't take this away from him either.

"Well, if we're going to have a dog, you're going to have to build a fence. I don't want to be those people who let their dog just wander loose. It's not safe for the dog, and Lord knows, Maddie would follow one anywhere."

Holt brightened. "I'll make sure you won't regret it."

"What kind of dog is she, anyway?"

"Some kind of yellow lab/shepherd mix, I think. I'll get her into the vet ASAP to confirm she's spayed. She's not a puppy, and it looks like she's already had at least one litter. The guys at the co-op are pegging her at about four or five years old."

"Well, hopefully that will make her easier to house-train."

The backdoor opened and girl and dog came bounding in.

"Mommy! Meet Banana Bread!"

The dog skidded to a halt inches away from Cayla and

slowly lowered to her haunches, as if sensing she was the one who had to be impressed. Cocking her head and peering up with liquid eyes, she lifted one paw. If Cayla hadn't already been sold, that would've toppled her.

Taking the paw, she gently shook it. "Welcome to the family, BB."

10

Holt had spent most of his military career getting up well before the ass crack of dawn. From basic training to PT to missions, there was always something keeping him from lolling around in bed, so the prospect of more of the same as a professional baker hadn't fazed him much. Not until those hours meant leaving a still sleeping Cayla behind. He liked being cuddled up with her, feeling the easy rise and fall of her breathing. And he liked being around for the morning routine of getting Maddie up and off to school. Starting his day off with both their smiles was like being injected with a little shot of sunshine. Plus, his help meant Cayla was a bit less rushed. A little less stressed.

But work was work, and he'd made promises to his partners before he'd made vows to his wife, so he hauled his ass in to the bakery well before the dark and early to help stock their cases for the limited run they had planned for the day. In honor of BB, he made banana nut muffins, along with lemon poppyseed scones, and a cinnamon streusel coffeecake he suspected was going to fly off the shelves when they opened at 7:30. It was still in the oven when he stripped off his apron.

"Hey, can you take care of that coffee cake? It's got another twenty minutes before it needs to come out. I'm gonna run home to help Cayla get Maddie off to school. I'll be back as soon as we get her dropped off."

"No worries. Tell the missus we said hi." Jonah batted his long-lashed eyes.

Brax thumped him on the arm. "Hey, we can handle the morning rush if you and Cayla want to take advantage of that empty house."

"Are we really making excuses so he can bang his wife?"

Brax rolled his eyes. "You're a pig. And at this point, yeah. I feel flat sorry for him. They didn't get a kidless honeymoon."

"Our perpetually interrupted love life is none of your business, although thanks for the offer. She's got a client meeting early, so no time for a post-school-drop-off tryst."

"Did he really just say, 'tryst?'" Jonah wanted to know.

"I don't even want to know what you'd call it. I'll be back." Leaving his friends bickering in the kitchen, he bagged a few of the muffins and headed for home.

Brax's suggestion wasn't a bad one. They both ran their own businesses. If they could just schedule a block of uninterrupted time while Maddie was in school... Well, he could think of a million and one erotic ways to spend it.

Satisfied with the idea and intent on planting that little seed in Cayla's head before they went their separate ways for the day, Holt was smiling as he slid out of the driver's seat.

Then he opened the kitchen door and walked into absolute pandemonium.

Maddie was sobbing. Cayla had her hand fisted in BB's ruff, her own eyes red-rimmed as she struggled to wrestle the dog back outside. The smell. Dear God, the smell. BB had unquestionably been skunked. Holt crossed over, registering that he was sloshing through water coming from... somewhere.

He opened his mouth to ask what happened, but shut it

again when he saw Cayla's face. She was barely holding it together, and he recognized that one more thing was going to send her over the edge. Instead, he scooped Maddie up, sniffing to see if the skunk had gotten her, too. Just the hands, probably from petting BB.

He sat her on the counter and pointed. "Stay. And don't touch anything."

From Maddie's room, he grabbed the dog crate, tossing out the bed and carrying the whole thing straight out the back door. Cayla followed him out, nudging BB into it and shutting her in.

She straightened, shoving her hair out of her face with the back of a hand. Her shoulders shook. "I have a client meeting in forty minutes. Maddie's going to be late for school. All I wanted was the chance to refinish that table and chairs for the office this afternoon, so I can finally have clients come there instead of going to them. And now..." Her voice choked.

Holt's brain was already running scenarios, prioritizing tasks. Mission prerogative: Keep his wife from crying. "Do we have hydrogen peroxide?"

She sniffled. A dangerous sound. "I... yes. In the bathroom, under the sink."

He bolted to the back, snagging the hydrogen peroxide and hurrying back to the kitchen. As the only one who hadn't touched skunked dog fur, he dug through the cabinet for the baking soda and dish soap, mixing up a quick batch of de-skunking solution. They'd need more for the dog, but she wasn't the top priority. Scooping Maddie up with one arm, he carried her to the sink and helped her wash and dry her hands before doing another sniff test. She was gonna need a change of clothes.

"Wash your hands and arms with that," Holt told Cayla. "I'll get her changed."

"I don't wanna change!" Maddie wailed in a register that

reminded him of nothing so much as an incoming mortar round.

"No choice, baby girl. You smell like skunk. Nobody at school wants to sniff that."

"But this shirt is my f... f... favorite!"

He eyed the sleeping sloth across the front of her t-shirt. Last week, the favorite had been one with unicorns. He supposed it was a kid's prerogative to change her mind. "We'll get it washed, and you can wear it tomorrow." Adding that to his mental to do list, he stripped the shirt up and off, grabbing the nearest one that came to hand and helping her into it.

"I don't like this shirt!"

Struggling for patience himself, Holt crouched down. "Bumblebee, sometimes we have to do things in life we don't like. Today is one of those days. Your mom is having a hard day already, and we don't need to make it worse, okay?"

Maddie rolled into a magnificent pout, but the tears stopped, so he was calling it a win. He scooped her up again, grabbing her backpack on the way through the living room and sloshing back into the kitchen. Cayla still stood at the kitchen sink.

"Do you need to change?"

"Probably."

"Go do that. I'll get her buckled in."

Bypassing the Camry, he settled Maddie into the car seat he'd bought for the 4-Runner, tucking the backpack and lunchbox at her feet.

"I'll be right back. Do not unbuckle that seatbelt."

Back inside, he paused to verify the source of the water. Something had busted on the dishwasher. A hose. Or maybe the door seal. He wouldn't know for sure until he got it pulled out. It was a damned good thing the floors in here were tiled. Grabbing up a stack of the second string towels from the laundry room, he dumped them at the edge of the room to contain the water until he could get back and deal with it.

Cayla was in the closet, pulling on a fresh blouse. Her movements were brittle, her hands shaking.

Holt cornered her inside, stroking his palms down her arms. "Take a breath."

The glare she shot him was clearly meant to vaporize.

"I've got Maddie. I'll take her to school. You go on to your client meeting."

"I need to reschedule. The dishwasher—"

"I'll handle it."

"And the dog—"

"I brought her into this household. I'm responsible for her. I'll take care of the bath and whatever else is necessary. Seriously, you need to get the hell out of here and let it all go for the rest of the day. I'll take care of all this."

"You have work, too."

"I have two business partners who can cover me. You don't. Let me do this. Go do what you need to do. I'll pick Maddie up from school this afternoon, and you can still get your painting time in. We can trade off after that so I can get to the custom order on my plate today."

"But—"

"No buts. You're not in this alone anymore, okay? I've got your back, and I'm taking all this off your plate. Now go or you'll be late for your meeting."

She opened her mouth, clearly intending to argue again, but he simply laid a finger over her lips.

"Go, Cayla. And I don't want to hear or see you until later this afternoon, okay?"

After a long, searching look, she relented. "Okay. Thank you."

He saw her off and joined Maddie in the 4-Runner, realizing he'd forgotten to give Cayla her muffins. *Bigger priorities.*

Turning in the driver's seat, he passed one back to Maddie. "Have a banana bread muffin. It'll make you feel better."

She gave him a side eye she'd clearly learned from her mother, but bit into the muffin. "Mmm. Can I have two?"

"If you finish the first one and there's time before we get to school."

He backed out of the driveway and put in a call to Brax on the SUV's Bluetooth as he headed into town to the elementary school.

"Calling for that extra time off after all?"

"Not like you think. The situation at home has gone entirely FUBAR." Holt outlined what he'd walked in on. "I'm about to drop Maddie at school and then go deal with the rest of this. I'm not gonna make it back in until later."

Brax made a low whistle. "That is an impressive level of FUBAR. We've got you covered, man. And let us know if we can do anything to help."

"Appreciate it." He hung up and turned onto Main Street.

"I want my other muffin."

Holt stretched his arm to hand it back to her.

"Thank you."

She made more yum noises as she bit into the second one, and he gave himself a mental pat on the back for diverting that disaster.

"Holt?"

"Yeah, kiddo?"

"What's FUBAR?"

Misty tucked a pencil into the twist of auburn hair knotted at her nape, dislodging some of the yellow freesia she wore today to advertise her wares. "Okay, I'll get to work on some designs this week and try to pull something together for you by next Thursday."

"Thanks. I really appreciate it." Cayla began gathering her own notes from this morning's client meeting. It had run long but had gone well. She'd landed the gig for planning the Sandersons' golden anniversary party. Since she'd already been in town from that, she went ahead and stopped by Moonbeams and Sweet Dreams to talk to her friend about prospective flowers.

"Now, how about you tell me why you've looked on the verge of tears since you walked in here?" She shot a look toward the front of the store, verifying they were alone. "Is everything going okay with... stuff?"

Appreciating the concern and the discretion, Cayla slumped in her chair. "So far, everything's been relatively quiet. No real problems there. At least none we didn't expect." Though she'd have felt better if her FBI contact had provided more information than, "We're working on it."

"The day just started as a total poop parade." She gave Misty the rundown of the terrible, horrible, no good, very bad day.

"Wow. That's a special level of awful, right there."

"I wouldn't have made my meeting at all if Holt hadn't come home to help get Maddie off to school. He shooed me out of the house and said he'd take care of everything. I was ordered not to think about it, but that's like telling me not to breathe. So I'm about to head back to the house to get things sorted."

"You don't think he meant it?"

"Oh, he's absolutely well-intentioned, but I don't think there's a snowball's chance in heck the day can be pulled out of the nosedive it took straight out of the gate. For my own sanity, I need the chaos rectified. Right now, I'm just hoping he at least managed to de-skunk the dog."

"Fair. How are things going with married life? Big adjustment?"

"Not as much of one as I expected. He's gone out of his way to be accommodating, and he's fantastic with Maddie."

"As previously documented." Misty leaned closer. "I'm more interested in how he is with you. After the reception, it seemed like you two were getting along... well." She only smirked a little.

Cayla's brain supplied a helpful replay of their little bathroom interlude from earlier in the week. She shivered. "We'd be getting along a lot better if not for a profound case of kiddus interruptus. I love my child. I adore my child. But I seriously wish she would sleep through the night in her own bed in her own room."

"Sounds like you need to invoke the time-honored tradition of parents everywhere."

"What's that?"

"Sleepover at grandma's house."

"Mama already takes on so much to help with her. I can't ask her to take Maddie overnight just so that I can jump my hot new husband. Especially as she's aware this wasn't exactly a love match."

"I mean, you don't have to *say* that's why you're asking."

"My mom is not a stupid woman. She'll know. And that's just... awkward."

"Cayla, honey, you gave birth. Your mom knows you've had sex at least once."

"I know, but... this is different. This was a marriage of convenience. Almost a business arrangement."

"It's still a marriage. She won't think less of you for treating it as such. Hell, I think most women *would* think less of you for *not* taking advantage of being married to someone like him."

Cayla snorted.

"I'm just saying," Misty continued, "married people have needs. It's worth thinking about."

Maybe after the specter of disaster had stopped hovering over her head. "Fair enough. I'm gonna head on home and do whatever's left that needs doing. Catch up soon, okay?"

She made the short drive, pulling into the garage with a deep sense of foreboding. Holt wasn't here. Was he out picking up some kind of supplies or had he needed to get back to the bakery? What level of chaos was waiting for her inside? Already wishing for an entire bottle of wine, she got out of the car.

The rumble of the washer greeted her as she stepped into the house. Washing whatever clothes and towels had come into contact with the skunk spray was smart. She didn't smell a trace of it as she moved into the kitchen. The dry, sparkling kitchen. She stopped in the middle of the floor and stared. There was no sign of the flood she'd left behind. But there was a note on the kitchen table, beside a stack of painting supplies and a bag from the hardware store.

Hope your meeting went well. BB is having an afternoon play date with Leno over at Mia and Brax's in their fenced-in backyard while she dries off from her bath. The seal on the dishwasher door has been replaced. Started the skunk load in the washer. If it finishes while you're home, you'll probably want to switch it to the dryer. Picked up the new lock at the hardware store when I went to get the seal. I'll get it installed when I get home. Happy painting.

Holt

Cayla read the note through twice, not quite believing it.

He'd taken care of everything, exactly as he'd promised. No muss, no fuss. No putting it off until later. He'd just done it. And she actually had time to finish painting her table and chairs for the office, exactly as he'd said she would.

She'd officially married a unicorn.

Drowning in gratitude, she burst into loud, messy tears.

God, this man. He paid attention. He saw what needed doing, anticipated the best course of action, and took care of business. Without her having to ask. Without her having to feel like she'd failed. All these years on her own, she'd been the one who had to see, anticipate, and tend. But he made her feel seen and taken care of, and she didn't quite know what to do with that. She kept expecting to wake up from this dream. And during all the moments when she knew she was awake, a part of her kept waiting for him to regret his impulsive offer of marriage as protection. Because he was too good to be true and there had to be something that made him real.

Despite the tears, she didn't waste the afternoon he'd given her. In two uninterrupted hours, she'd finished a second and final coat of paint on the table and entire set of chairs. As soon as they dried, they could haul them to her office and put them in place. Flushed with a sense of accomplishment and more relaxed than she'd been in weeks, Cayla changed again and drove up to the bakery to pick up her daughter.

Knowing the front door would be locked, she walked along the wrap-around porch to the service entrance, noting the faint thump of music. Holt was rocking out to something while he worked, that was for sure. She tugged open the door and got blasted with sound. Maddie sat on one of the worktables, her smile radiant as she boogied in place while Holt belted out "Can't Stop The Feeling." Cayla propped her shoulder against the door frame, enjoying his damned fine impression of Justin Timberlake, using a whisk as a microphone. And as he shook his ass and shimmied his shoulders, to the absolute delight of her daughter, she felt her heart simply thud to the floor at his feet.

She'd been in lust with this man for months. In very heavy like with him almost as long. But now, she understood she was unquestionably, irrevocably, in love with him. Her friend. Her co-parent. Her husband.

Still absorbing the implications of that, she wasn't prepared when he snagged her hand and spun her into the dance. He just wrapped his arms around her, blue eyes sparkling as he continued to sing, until she fell into his rhythm and began to dance, too. She was laughing by the end, going to her toes to steal a kiss. He lingered, even as Maddie clapped her hands and begged for another song.

"Get your painting done?"

"I did." She curled a lock of his hair around her finger. "Thank you for being my hero today."

"You're welcome."

"I came to collect the munchkin so you can get to your custom order."

"I want another song!"

Cayla peered past Holt's shoulder. "You'll have to content yourself with me, baby. Holt's got work to do. And we need to go pick up Banana Bread from Mia's."

Maddie wrinkled her nose. "I hope she smells better."

"She does," Holt assured them. "Unless there's a vengeful skunk stalking the neighborhood."

"Let's just not put that idea out into the Universe. One close encounter of the odiferous kind is my quota for a lifetime. C'mon, sweetheart. Get your stuff."

Maddie hopped off the table and scurried into the office.

"I'll probably be late getting home. The cake's in the oven now, and it's still got to cool completely before I can start decorating. I'll do my best to make it for bath and bedtime."

Cayla really loved hearing him call them home. She wondered if it was part of the role he was playing or if he really felt that way. She intended to do everything in her power to make sure it was the latter. To that end, she herded her child toward the door and waved goodbye.

She had plans for her very good man.

11

Holt didn't make it home for bath or bedtime. It was nearing nine by the time he finally rolled up to the house. But the cake was finished, and it was damned fine work, if he did say so himself. He liked the challenge and precision of design. It gave him another use for the steady hands he'd so often turned to diffusing explosives.

He found Cayla on the sofa in the living room, a mostly empty glass of wine at her elbow and her e-reader in hand. Her bare toes had been painted a bright poppy red. Something about the sight of them made him smile. Maybe because the fact that she'd had time to do them meant the evening had gone smoothly. Her honey blonde hair was loose around her shoulders, and she seemed to be wearing—was that one of his button-down shirts?—with a pair of sleep shorts. She looked relaxed and comfortable. A far cry from where she'd started the day.

Her lips curved as he came into the room. "Get the cake finished?"

"Yeah. They'll be by to pick it up tomorrow."

"Good." She tipped back the last of her wine and set the e-reader aside.

"Maddie go down okay? I'm sorry I missed bedtime." Strange how fast he'd become accustomed to the routine. How he'd missed it.

"She's not here."

Holt froze in place, going on alert. He knew nothing was wrong, or Cayla would be losing her mind. No, this was something else.

She rose from the sofa and padded toward him. "I called in a favor and arranged a sleepover at my mother's for the entire weekend. Because I have plans for you, and I don't want to be interrupted. Again."

Fire sparked in his blood as she closed the distance between them. "Where's the dog?"

"Turns out being skunked, bathed, and having an all-day play date with Leno wore her out. She's been passed out in her crate for about an hour."

"Good to know. So you've got plans, huh?"

"Mmm."

That purr of sound had the blood already draining from his head. He wanted to hear more of it as he peeled her out of that shirt and tasted every sweet curve of her body.

Tone conversational, she trailed her fingers across his chest, gently nudging him backward, toward the hall. "I thought you were gorgeous before I knew you. That was surface."

Those fingers reached for the bottom of his t-shirt, sliding it up. "Add to that, we have chemistry. Really great chemistry. But that's just biology."

The shirt got stuck somewhere around his pecs, so he helped her out, dragging it off with one hand and letting it fall. Her eyes skated over his bare chest, going dark as they took in his tattoos before coming back to his face.

"Then I got to know you, and I discovered that dry wit, which is my favorite kind of humor."

They passed into the bedroom. She'd installed the lock he'd bought, not that it looked like they'd need it tonight. One of the bedside lamps was on low. It cast just enough light to see the hint of cleavage where the shirt she'd robbed gaped open. His fingers itched to touch, but he kept them to himself for a little while longer, understanding she was going somewhere with all this.

"Then I saw you fall in love with my daughter. A major plus in my book." She backed him up until his knees hit the bed. "And there's that amazing, selfless willingness to help with literally anything, which I can promise you, is reason enough to make most women swoon."

"Most?" He arched a brow, sitting as she nudged him down. "Not you?"

"Oh, it was a near thing, for sure. And I have a multitude of different ways I'd love to show my appreciation for all that. But it was really the JT that did it."

Holt huffed a laugh, unable to resist gripping her hips. "Yeah? The singing?"

Her hands slid around his shoulders as she climbed up to straddle his lap. "That, and I really need to know what you can do with these hips without an audience."

He pulled her down tight against his erection, loving the little whimper she made as he flexed against her. "All weekend, you said?"

"Mom's got Maddie until Sunday afternoon, and I have no events and no meetings on the calendar until Monday afternoon because I cleared Monday morning for the grand opening. Consider it our honeymoon."

Hell to the yes.

He started to kiss her, but she laid a finger over his lips, her expression turning serious.

"I just want to make it clear, in case it's not already, that this is not about gratitude for what you've been doing for me or for Maddie—though God knows, I can't imagine anyone else leaping in like you have. It's not somehow transactional. I want *you*. I wanted you almost from the moment we met, and I've only wanted you more since. I'm choosing *you* for however long this lasts. I just needed you to know that."

However long this lasts.

What would she say if he told her he wanted to make it real? That he didn't want to end this whenever the threat of Raynor was resolved? That he was in love with her?

It was too much, too soon. She'd said she didn't trust easy. Never mind that being with her was the easiest thing he'd ever done. He wouldn't risk what he'd found with her by pushing for more than she was ready for. He wouldn't push her at all. She needed to come around to the idea that this marriage was right in her own time.

But he could show her.

Combing both hands through all that silky hair, he drew her mouth to his. The taste of her hit him like a double shot of top-shelf whiskey, and he had to remind himself not to gulp, not to rush. This need had been building between them for weeks. Months, really. She'd made sure they'd have the time to savor each other, so by damn, he'd deliver.

One by one, he released the buttons down the front of her shirt, slowly baring her shoulders, her chest. He explored each new piece of her with lazy, lingering kisses as he palmed her breasts, rolling her nipples between his fingers. She rocked against him, restless and needy, draining all the blood and a lot of his good intentions out of his head. If she kept that up, he was going to blow like a teenaged boy on prom night.

Wanting to last longer than that, he leaned back and rolled, until her back was pressed to the mattress and he could slide off the end. Her hair was already mussed, her lips rosy and swollen from his. He wanted to see what else was flushed and swollen for him. Hooking his fingers in the waistband of her sleep shorts, he dragged them down, taking the underwear with them, until she was bare to him. She wasn't shy, didn't curl up or hide. She simply lay back and let him look his fill. And God, she was stunning.

Snagging her by the ankles, he dragged her to the edge of the bed, wrangling a laugh from her. At least until he knelt and pressed her knees apart. Her laugh turned to a moan as he took a long, slow lick up her center. So damned sweet and already drenched. On a growl, he lowered his head and feasted. He'd been thinking about what she'd taste like, what she'd sound like when he took her like this, and he wasn't disappointed. Her unmistakable cries of pleasure echoed through the room as he drove her up and up, until she shattered on a scream that was the best thing he'd heard in forever.

As he eased her down from the peak, she rolled her head toward him, panting. "I can't even be annoyed about that cocky smirk on your face. Because... damn."

His grin only broadened. "I think I understand now why you were so reluctant to get up to anything with Maddie in the house. You're a screamer."

Cayla dropped her head back, covering her face with both hands. "I mean, it's been six years. I've got some pent up... needs."

Six years. So no one since her ex. An unreasonable sense of possession and satisfaction shot through him at that. He wanted to claim every inch of her as his. That was just one more reason to take his time.

Holt dragged her hands down so he could look into her eyes. "Don't be embarrassed. I fucking love it."

Those eyes darkened, and a feline smile curved her lips. "Then why don't you come up here and let's see exactly how much you can make me scream?"

SOMEHOW CAYLA FOUND the muscle control to scoot back on the bed, leaving room for Holt to join her. He kept his eyes on hers as he lowered the zipper and eased the cargo pants and boxers down just enough to free his erection. She wanted to wrap her hands around the proud, thick jut of it, but she wasn't quite sure how to handle this part of the proceedings, so she waited to take her cues from him. He turned his back to her, giving her a view of his magnificent ass as he sat and worked off his clothes. The outer sleeve of his prosthesis came all the way up his thigh. He rolled it down, carefully extracting his leg and setting the artificial limb aside. Then he rolled down the inner sleeve, and she spotted the deep groove on the outside of his leg. Up 'til now, he'd been very careful to shield her, always wearing shorts or undressing in the dark, but there was no hiding the scarring that told a story of incredible violence and pain.

She didn't realize she'd gasped until his shoulders bunched.

"Shrapnel." The word was clipped and brusque, ripe with unspoken horrors.

Not wanting to reopen that wound, Cayla crawled down to him, skimming her hands across those rock-hard shoulders, following with a slow trail of kisses. "Come to bed, warrior mine."

He twisted to search her face. She held his gaze, letting all the raw heat and hunger show in her face because the last thing she wanted was for him to mistake her compassion for pity or disgust. At last, his shoulders relaxed, and he tipped her back with a wicked glint in his eyes.

Slowly, so maddeningly slowly, he kissed his way up the length of her body, starting at her ankles. Those nibbling kisses lit little fires in their wake, adding layer upon layer of sensation with each inch higher. At the juncture of her thighs, he took a detour that had her bucking and desperate.

"Oh God, I'm so close."

"Good." The heat of that one smug syllable against her center had her quivering at the edge.

She tightened her hand in his hair and tugged a little. "No. I want you inside me this time. Come here."

For once, he followed orders, climbing the rest of the way up her body and reaching for a condom from the box on the bedside table. He rolled it on, giving his erection a testing stroke.

"Mine," she breathed.

The corners of his mouth tipped up. "Yes, ma'am."

He settled between her thighs, bracing himself above her with an arm on either side of her shoulders. Cayla loved having the weight of him over her, feeling him surrounding her. She reached between them, finally getting her hand on him as she guided him to her entrance and lifted her hips. "Now. Please."

Face a mask of concentration, he pressed inside her, and she lost her breath. She was wet and so ready, but he was big.

"Okay?"

"So okay," she gasped. "Don't stop."

He sank the rest of the way in, and she cried out at the sensation of him filling her up, her body arching in search of more. Then he began to move. A gloriously slow advance and retreat, going a little deeper with every stroke until he hit some vital point and made her shatter.

She was still shuddering when he rolled to his back, taking her with him so she straddled his hips. Dizzy, delirious from pleasure, she gasped again as he continued to move, his hands gripping her thighs.

"Ride me," he ordered, and damn if that bossy tone didn't have her body climbing again.

She could see him better from here, watch his face as she

moved, learning what drew out that gasping growl. His eyes were blue flames on hers as she dragged her hands up her torso to cup her breasts, rolling her nipples as he'd done.

"Cayla." He groaned her name, and it sounded as much like a prayer as a plea.

It had been so damned long since she'd felt like a woman. Since she'd felt desired. And she'd never felt wanted like this.

His exquisite control was starting to fray. She could feel it in the tightening of his grip, holding her tighter against him as his movements shifted in rhythm, holding longer inside her before he drew back and thrust again. A wave building, building as it got closer to shore.

He came on a roar, his head thrown back, the tendons in his neck cording. The pulse of him inside her tipped her impossibly over the edge again, into delicious madness.

Sweaty, exhausted, Cayla simply wilted down over his chest. It heaved as much as hers. From some deep reserve, he found enough energy to wrap his arms around her, turning his head to kiss her cheek. That little gesture of tenderness made her heart flutter, and she cuddled against him, basking in the sensation of closeness.

They lay in silence for a long time. So long, Cayla wondered if he'd fallen asleep. Summoning the last dregs of energy, she lifted her head a few inches to peer down at him.

His eyes were open and on her, the corners crinkled with a smile. "Well, I think we're going to have to make some investment in soundproofing."

She damned well wasn't going to apologize for enjoying herself and him. "You're lucky I don't have the energy to smack you."

"That wasn't a criticism. I'm going to need to make you do that again as many times as possible."

More than mollified, she folded her hands on his chest and rested her chin on them. "While I am fully in support of this plan, we're going to have to get creative. New lock aside, we still have a very adorable cock blocker in the house."

Holt stroked a hand down her spine, ending with a proprietary squeeze of her butt. "I'm extremely motivated."

"I am extremely hungry. I say we clean up and go forage before taking all possible advantage of the time we've been given."

"I might have brought something home from the bakery. Why don't you go check. I'll be along shortly."

Understanding he needed a few minutes, she kissed him soundly and scooted off the bed. After a quick trip to the bathroom, she headed for the kitchen, grabbing Holt's t-shirt off the floor and slipping it on. From the crate in Maddie's room, Banana Bread stirred.

Her gold and black tail wagged as Cayla came in. "Guess we woke you. No surprise there. I'd apologize, but I'm really not sorry at all."

BB trailed her into the kitchen, where she found a bakery box on the counter and pounced on it like a kid. Nestled inside was a stack of sugar-dusted lemon bars.

"Unicorn," she murmured.

Lifting two out, she carried them with her as she opened the back door and stepped out onto the porch. The dog dashed into the yard and began to sniff.

"Stay close. We aren't gonna have a repeat of this morning."

While she waited for BB to do her business, Cayla took a huge bite. The tart, sweet buttery goodness melted on her tongue, dragging out another moan.

"Getting started on another round without me?"

"Hush, I'm having a religious experience here." She shoved the rest of the bar into her mouth as she turned.

Holt stood framed in the doorway. The cut-off sweatpants he wore hung low on his hips, leaving the v-grooves on either side of his six-pack abs exposed. The sight had her mouth watering for a whole other reason. He strode out to join her, bending to skim his lips along her throat before taking a bite of the other lemon bar in her hand.

"These are amazing."

"I had some time on my hands while I was waiting for the cake to cool. I know chocolate is Maddie's favorite, but I was taking a guess that lemon is yours."

"Good guess." She took another greedy bite, sighing with utter contentment. "How many calories do you suppose orgasms burn?"

"No idea. We could probably google it."

"Nah." As BB trotted by them to go back inside, she tapped his cheek. "You just have to give me enough of them to counter all the baked goods you keep bringing home."

His eyes crinkled again. "We'll consider it one of the unspoken vows."

Cayla's heart gave a lurch. She'd made vows to this man. All the love, honor, and cherish ones. She hadn't given a lot of consideration to them at the time, all her focus being on the end goal of protecting Maddie. But they scrolled through her mind again now because she found she meant them. She wanted this marriage and everything that went with it. And as she stood with him under the spring stars, it felt entirely possible that he just might, too.

Back in the kitchen, BB waited patiently for a dog biscuit. Cayla dug one out of the jar. "Good girl." The dog nipped it neatly out of her hand, then took herself back off to bed.

"Well, I guess she's still tired. Or maybe she doesn't want a front-row seat to the rest of our shenanigans."

"Shenanigans, huh?" Holt grinned and grabbed them both another lemon bar.

"Shenanigans. Debauchery. Sexcapades." She shrugged. "Pick one."

"Oh, I definitely like sexcapades."

Nibbling on the half a lemon bar he passed her, she mused, "I wonder how many fantasies we can squeeze into the next thirty-six hours."

"I'd say that depends on what those fantasies are. Throw some out there." He shoved the rest of the lemon bar in his mouth.

"Wall sex." She blurted it out before thinking better of it. "I don't know if the mechanics are practical or—"

Holt smirked again. "So, the thing about being an amputee is that it's in my best interest to keep in peak physical condition. It helps with all sorts of things." He stalked closer, skimming his hands down her back to grip her thighs. "Strength." He lifted her until she wrapped her legs around his waist, where she could feel that he was more than ready for round two. "Balance." He carried her effortlessly into the living room, toward the nearest empty wall. "Endurance."

She gasped as he trapped her between the wall and the hard, muscled length of his body. "I am a fan of all of these things."

"Then grab the condom in my pocket and let's start the count at one."

Delighted, aroused, Cayla could only think that no matter how many they got through, in the end her ultimate fantasy was him.

12

"Well, somebody clearly had a good weekend."
Without missing a beat, Holt flipped Jonah
off and continued to sing along with "Here
Comes The Sun" as he spread fresh strawberry jam over the
breakfast bars he'd be sliding in the oven shortly.

Still smirking, Jonah came on inside the bakery kitchen and
moved to the second set of ovens, setting them to preheat. "Are
we really gonna be listening to this tooth-rotting sweet playlist
this morning?"

"When you get here first, you can pick the tunes."

He'd never been more grateful for his training to function
on little to no sleep. He and Cayla hadn't wasted a single
moment of their honeymoon staycation weekend, which meant
he hadn't gotten started on his wares for the grand opening
until the very wee hours of Monday morning. Absolutely
worth it.

Across the room, Jonah tipped out the big plastic bin of
bread dough he'd prepped last night, punching it down and
dividing the dough up for boules. Holt added the top layer of
oat mixture to his breakfast bars and slid them into one of the

waiting ovens as The New Beatles rolled into Pharrell Williams' "Happy."

Brax stepped through the back door and stared. "I'm sorry. Who are you and what have you done with our generally grumpy friend?"

"Apparently, the secret to improving his mood was getting him laid."

"I mean, he's breathing and a dude, so that's hardly a surprise. I've certainly got more pep in my step after a very happy send off from my wife this morning."

"You're both assholes," Jonah complained.

"I'd say we're both happily married men." Brax set his travel mug of coffee down and headed for the walk-in cooler. "That is what we're seeing here, right? You're really happy with Cayla?"

Holt took a long glug from his bottle of water. "I am. I mean, I didn't expect it to be awful. I like her and Maddie both. But I didn't expect it to be quite so..."

"Real?" Brax suggested.

"Yeah."

Jonah put the trays of shaped boules to one side to rise. "You don't think this is just a product of close proximity and the situation?"

Holt gave the question real consideration. "No. I think the close proximity and situation just got me over whatever reservations I had about getting involved with her on the front end. I suppose, in a weird way, I almost owe her ex a thank you for getting me here."

"That's twisted." Brax began to roll out the brick of puff pastry he'd pulled from the cooler. "Anything new on that front?"

"No. It's been too quiet." And he needed to pull his head out of this honeymoon haze and turn his attention back to that problem. The last thing they needed was to get blindsided.

Jonah shrugged. "Maybe your little caveman possessive

routine actually worked."

"Maybe. But that doesn't fit with the personality Cayla's described for the guy. Feels more like he's biding his time. For what, I don't know. If he really is planning on raising a custody suit, it takes time to pull that together, I guess. So we're just waiting and watching."

Brax clapped Holt on the shoulder. "No matter how you got here, marriage and family look good on you, man."

Marriage and family. Two things he hadn't thought he'd want after how he'd grown up. But he couldn't imagine going back to life without Cayla or her delightfully impish daughter. He could even see them with another one.

"Why do you suddenly look like you've been poleaxed?"

Blinking at Jonah, Holt just shook his head. Another kid was getting way the hell ahead of things. It was just the weekend of stupendous sex talking. Or something. They'd been married for less than three weeks. He hadn't even convinced Cayla that she wanted forever with him yet. There'd be time enough to discuss the prospect of expanding their family later, when the threat to Maddie was definitively over.

Needing to get his mind on something else, he headed to the cooler for more eggs and milk. There were popovers to be made.

The three of them lost themselves in the familiar rhythm of baking, navigating around each other as if they'd been working together for years. By the time 7:30 rolled around, their glass cases were full and the shelves behind were loaded with fresh bread.

"All right. Let's do it." Holt held out a fist to each of them for a bump.

Brax took up position behind the cases, and Holt stood at the register as Jonah threw open the door.

"Good morning, Eden's Ridge! Come get your carbs on."

"Don't mind if we do."

For a moment, Jonah's mouth went slack. Then his eyes lit up as Rachel McCleary strode inside, accompanied by a familiar redhead.

"Well, aren't y'all a sight for sore eyes?"

"No way were we going to miss your grand opening. How are you, Jonah?" Dr. Audrey Graham, the brain behind the therapy program that had saved them all, laughed as he wrapped her in a hug. "I'm guessing that's good?"

"Absolutely." His attention shifted to Rachel. "You didn't tell me you were coming back down."

The tall, willowy blonde shrugged and offered an unrepentant smile. "Surprise. We had to come offer our support." She moved in for a hug herself.

Jonah pulled her in, and Holt didn't miss how he curved around her, his expression softening as he turned his face into her hair.

When the hell was his buddy going to make a move? Holt had been wondering for more than a year. It was obvious Jonah felt something for their widowed teacher. It was equally obvious her affection for him surpassed what she showed the rest of them. Then again, with the distance between Tennessee and where she lived in Syracuse, maybe Jonah had decided against it. Long distance was hell.

Still, this was the second trip Rachel had made down here, and Holt was willing to bet it wouldn't be her last.

He slipped out from behind the counter to give Audrey a hug himself. "You definitely need a tour. These two jokers can handle the crowd for a minute."

The overall decibel level had already risen dramatically as people streamed in after the women.

While Rachel slipped behind the counter to greet Brax, Holt took Audrey back, feeling a glow of pride as he showed off their kitchen.

"How long are you two here?"

"Just a couple of days. We have to get back to the program. But we wanted to come support you guys. We're so proud of all of you."

"We wouldn't be here without the two of you. Whatever you want that's on offer is yours. Your money's no good here."

"That's hardly good business." But she smiled.

"Jonah and Brax will back me up on this. We're grateful, Doc."

Her cheeks pinked with pleasure and pride. "And I understand congratulations are in order. You eloped?"

"Been talking to Rachel, huh?"

She laughed. "Of course."

Holt knew Jonah had been keeping her up to date on the goings on with the three of them, but he had no idea exactly how much detail he might've gone into about the unusual circumstances around Holt's marriage. "I did. Nearly three weeks ago. Her name is Cayla, and she's awesome."

Rachel stuck her head through the wide pass-thru window. "Are we talking about your new bride? I want to know everything. I met her on my last trip down and adored her. She's got the cutest little girl."

Audrey's brows shot up. "Jumping on into fatherhood, huh?" There was no judgment in her tone. She was too good a therapist for that, but Holt still felt weird. She knew all about how he'd had to be the parent growing up, and how he hadn't ever intended to cross this bridge.

"Maddie's a sweetheart."

"She's also *extremely* disappointed to be missing the grand opening in favor of school." Cayla pushed through the swinging kitchen door and headed straight for him, rising to her toes to brush a quick kiss to his lips.

When she would have pulled back, Holt tightened his arm around her and lingered until she relaxed against him with a contented sigh. He eased back, exhaling one himself. "Hi."

"Good morning." There were faint smudges beneath her eyes, but the I've-seen-you-naked-and-plan-to-again-very-soon twinkle canceled them out.

"I gather this is she?"

Remembering there were other people around, Holt gave himself a mental kick. "Yeah. Cayla, I'd like you to meet Dr. Audrey Graham. Audrey, my wife, Cayla."

Audrey flashed a warm smile and offered her hand.

Cayla took it, beaming in return. "Pleased to meet you. I've heard so much about you and your program."

"I've been extremely fortunate to work with some really great guys. Your husband is one of the best."

Cayla cuddled into him. "I know."

Damn, if that didn't make Holt want to puff up his chest with pride.

"Oh my God, you two are the cutest!"

"Rachel! You're back."

Suddenly there were a lot of women talking. Something about planning a celebration dinner later that night before Rachel and Audrey had to fly back to New York. Holt didn't quite follow the exchange, but he figured someone would tell him where to be when, and he'd just show up and be okay.

The front door burst open, banging back against the wall.

"Holt Christopher Steele, you've got some serious explaining to do!"

Everybody turned toward the tattooed brunette with purple streaks in her hair and a ferocious scowl on her face. As she stalked forward, hands curled to fists, people backed away, eying her nervously. Spotting him through the pass-thru, she made a beeline for the kitchen door, shoving it open and marching inside.

"Not only did you freaking *elope* without bothering to tell me, but I had to hear it from Cash Grantham instead of you! What do you have to say for yourself?"

He sighed in resignation. "Hi, sis."

Face a thundercloud, she poked him in the chest. "Don't you 'Hi, sis' me, you little shit."

Knowing there was only one way to deal with her, Holt bent and scooped her up, tossing her over his shoulder. "That's big shit to you."

Hadley shrieked and pounded his back. "Put me down, you oaf!"

"Not until you say it."

"Never!"

"Fine." He strode over and made as if to dump her in the trash can.

"Okay! Okay! Youarebigbrothersupreme!" Her shriek transitioned to an outright cackle as he flipped her back over and set her on her feet.

Holt was grinning as he absorbed her semi-tackle hug. "Hey, Squirt."

"Good to see you, Jerkface. I could have done without that particular walk down memory lane."

He caught her in a headlock. "Just be glad you're too tall for me to dangle by the ankles anymore. Now come meet the woman you're chewing my ass over."

Hadley gave him a none-too-soft punch in the kidneys, exactly as he'd taught her, and straightened, all good cheer as she glanced between Audrey, Cayla, and Rachel. "So which one of you married my uncommunicative brother?"

Audrey and Rachel pointed at a wide-eyed Cayla, who raised her hand.

Hadley barreled toward her, wrapping her in an enthusiastic hug. "I'm Hadley. Your sister-in-law. And I really hope this dumbass let you know I existed."

Cayla linked her arm through his sister's, arching a brow in his direction. "I feel like you and I have a lot to talk about."

As they both gave him the side-eye, Holt understood he was in big trouble.

~

"I HAVE A NIECE?" Hadley's voice was bright with excitement as she studied the photos on the wall.

That instant willingness to consider Maddie family had some of Cayla's nerves evaporating. "She's five."

"She's adorable."

Trailed by Banana Bread, Hadley continued to wander, gaze roving over the new photos Cayla had added to the collection over the past couple of weeks. Initially, it had been part of keeping up the image of a happy little family. But she'd enjoyed documenting how Holt had slid so seamlessly into their life, and she loved seeing his little flashes of surprise when he found them.

His sister picked up the one Misty had taken of their first dance. "I'm sorry I missed the wedding."

"It was small and fast. That was from our *Hey, we eloped!* party."

She set the picture down. "Why did you elope? Not a fan of big weddings?"

Cayla laughed. "I'm actually an event planner. Big weddings are kind of my jam. But I did that once already, and it ended badly. Something different this go round seemed sensible."

"Mmm." Hadley didn't have nearly the poker face her brother did. She was clearly trying to work her way around to something. Probably a polite way to ask what the hell they'd been thinking. Cayla couldn't blame her for that. Holt was, as far as she knew, Hadley's only remaining family. It made sense that she'd be protective of him.

"You don't approve."

Hadley winced. "Oh God, is that how I'm coming off? No.

Please don't think that I think that. I'm just surprised, is all. I didn't know he was seeing anybody at all, and I definitely would not have expected him to pick a single mom." She closed her eyes. "There I go, sticking my foot in it again. There is nothing wrong with single moms. It's just ours was one, and it was... complicated."

"Complicated how?"

The bright blue eyes that were so like her brother's fixed on Cayla. "Has Holt told you anything about what it was like for us growing up?"

"Just that he raised you. He didn't get into specifics about why." And she'd wondered more than a little about that.

Hadley blew out a breath. "We're gonna need fortification for this conversation."

Pulse quickening at the prospect of having her curiosity satisfied, Cayla determined to do what she could to smooth the conversation. "It's way too early for alcohol, but I've got a pint of Karamel Sutra in the freezer."

Her eyes crinkled, her smile flashing much more readily than Holt's usually did. "A Ben and Jerry's woman. I like your style."

They settled in the kitchen with bowls of ice cream.

Hadley crossed those enviably long legs and stabbed in her spoon. "So, we didn't have what you could call a great childhood. Our dad split right after I was born, and our mom was... devastated. I don't have any memories of him myself. Holt says he was no great prize. You know how some women just can't be alone? Like they're not complete without being attached to some guy? That was our mom. She was needy and clingy and, quite frankly, she couldn't hack it as a grownup, let alone as a parent. When she was in a relationship, she was happy, and she put all her attention there. When those inevitably failed— because she had complete shit taste in men—she fell into the bottle. Either way, her focus was never on us."

Hadley's delivery was matter-of-fact, but the image she painted absolutely bruised Cayla's heart. She couldn't imagine not putting Maddie first.

"So, Holt stepped in. He made sure I was fed and clothed, and got to school on time. He saw that the bills were paid—when she actually held down a job and there was money to pay them—and he did what was necessary so we could make ends meet when there wasn't, so social services didn't come knocking. He changed the diapers, handled the nightmares, and kissed the scraped knees. And he learned basically every Disney song ever written because it was the only thing that would distract me and calm me down when Mom was on a bender or fighting with her latest boyfriend."

Tears slid down Cayla's cheeks, and a warm weight settled on her knee. BB looked up at her with soulful brown eyes. She indulged her need for comfort by stroking those velvet-soft ears. "Sounds like he was an amazing brother."

"He was my fucking rock. But he was a parent from the time he was seven years old. He never said a word of complaint, but I wasn't blind. I knew that wasn't what he wanted. No kid wants that life. That responsibility. So the moment I was old enough to be out on my own, when I had a job and a safe place to stay, I told him it was his turn to do what he wanted. He enlisted. And I don't have any doubt he'd still be out there if that IED hadn't taken his foot and robbed him of his career. He never talked about retiring, settling down. The whole wife and family track wasn't on his radar. He already did the parent thing with me, so I'm just surprised to find him in this situation, is all."

No wonder he'd spent so much effort trying to resist their attraction. Of course, after that total lack of a childhood, he wouldn't actively choose to have an instant family. If not for Arthur, they'd never have gotten here. What the hell did that say about them?

Hadley laid a hand on hers. "Please don't take that as any

sort of criticism against you or your daughter. If you make him happy, that's the only thing that matters to me. And from everything I've seen, you do. I've never seen my brother look at another woman like he was looking at you today."

Oh, Cayla didn't doubt he had affection for her and Maddie both, and the attraction was a hundred percent real. But it was early days yet. So far, their unconventional marriage had been filled with mostly the easy and the fun. What happened when real life set in? When the daily grind and inevitable frustrations got to him, reminding him of all those responsibilities he'd finally been able to shed once before? She'd thought he'd have reason to regret their hasty marriage, and it looked like she was right. How long did they have before their little bubble of happiness burst and he wanted out?

The idea of it made her stomach curdle.

Hadley's face twisted in distress. "I'm so sorry. I've upset you. I shouldn't have said anything."

"No. No, I'm glad you did." She spooned up more ice cream but didn't actually taste it. "It's just..." Should she say anything? Holt hadn't told his sister about their marriage. Cayla didn't get the sense it was because he didn't trust her.

Hadley's eyes went wide. "Oh God. Are you pregnant? Was that why the big rush?"

"Pregnant?" Cayla's hand instinctively went to her belly, remembering the life she'd carried there. For a moment, the yearning for another was so strong, it stole her breath. She forced a laugh. "No. Definitely not pregnant. But you're right. There's more to our marriage than a simple elopement. We're... complicated."

They'd both wiped out the ice cream by the time Cayla finished explaining how her marriage to Holt had come about.

"Oh, that makes total sense. That's exactly the kind of thing my brother would do. He's got that hero streak that's fifteen miles wide. I guess that's why he didn't tell me."

Because it's not a real marriage.

Hadley didn't say it, but the implication was there. And that just made Cayla feel worse. Every doubt she'd harbored from the moment she'd said "I do" came back four-fold. Things were great between them right now, but that didn't mean it would stay that way. She understood that once Arthur was dealt with, once Maddie was safe, she'd have to let Holt go. His sister had, when the time had come. How could Cayla be selfish and ask any more of him than he'd already given?

"Okay, Bumblebee, it's time to get ready for bed."

Maddie and Hadley shot twin expressions of pleading Holt's way. "Noooo."

He couldn't hold back the smile. The two of them had been smitten with each other almost at first sight. No surprise there. Maddie reminded him so much of Hadley at that age. At least Hadley in her more carefree moments.

Cayla added her parental backup. "Sorry, Munchkin. School tomorrow. Say goodnight to Aunt Hadley."

Something was wrong. Holt could feel it. She'd been her usual charming, friendly self all afternoon and evening. Affectionate to him, to Maddie. The consummate hostess and friend during the celebratory dinner with everyone for the grand opening. The event planner who totally had all her shit together as she continued to discuss Brax and Mia's upcoming vow renewal. The excited friend when Mia offered to swing by tomorrow to help with some stuff at Cayla's office. But he knew something was off.

There hadn't been a moment to get her alone to talk to her, and his oblique query about whether she'd heard something more from Raynor had been met with a headshake, which could've as easily meant "Not now" as "No."

Happy as he was to see Hadley, he was ready to wrap this evening up so he could talk to his wife.

Maddie scuffed her toe on the carpet, frowning. "Stupid school. I miss all the fun things."

Hadley crouched down to her level. "I've got to go home tomorrow, but I promise I'll be back to visit. And we're totally going to talk on the computer, okay?"

"Okay!" Maddie threw herself into some kind of complicated handshake-fist bump routine. When had she had time to learn *that?*

The two of them exchanged big bear hugs, then Cayla took Maddie off to start the bath routine.

It was the first time he'd had a chance to talk to Hadley alone since she'd arrived. Wanting to give Cayla time to get fully engaged in bath time, he started off with brotherly picking.

"So what have you been doing hanging out with Cash?" He and Cash Grantham went way back, before the Army. He'd known Hadley as a kid, been there to help bail her out of her rebellious teen years. But Holt hadn't known the two of them had stayed in touch.

His sister shrugged. "He came in to get some fresh ink. I'm working on a half sleeve for him. We got to talking, and he's the one who brought up that you'd eloped, wanting to know what I thought about the whole thing."

Holt hadn't asked for any kind of NDA. He'd trusted his buddy had enough discretion as a security expert not to run his mouth. But he also hadn't expected Cash to be seeing anybody to whom the news would mean anything. "What else did he say?"

"He clammed the hell up when he found out that I didn't know anything. So I got my ass on a plane and came out here." Annoyance sharpened her tone. "The bigger question is why you didn't tell me yourself."

"That's complicated."

"Not so complicated. Cayla told me about her ex. It's a good thing, what you're doing for them."

Holt shook off the compliment. He didn't like looking at his marriage as the protection detail it had started as. "What did you say to her?"

"What are you talking about?"

He paused, listening down the hall. Cayla's low laugh accompanied faint sounds of splashing from the bathroom. "She's off. Something's wrong. She's acting like it's not, but something's wrong. What did you say to her?"

Hadley folded her arms, dark brows drawing together in insult. "I told her about mom and growing up and all the stuff you should have said to her yourself."

He swore. Now he understood why Cayla was upset. Knowing about his past would just remind her of his initial reluctance to get involved without duress. How much harder was he going to have to work to convince his wife that he was in love with her and he wanted this marriage to be real?

"I don't want to talk about that shit. It's over. It's done. That's it."

Hadley just leveled him with a flat stare. They both knew that their past was a huge part of what had made him who he was. But she didn't push.

"I'm gonna head on back to the inn. I'll stop by the bakery before I leave town tomorrow."

"See that you do." He wrapped her in a big hug, holding tight to the one person in the world who'd lived through the same hell he had and come out stronger. It was his proudest accomplishment that he'd been able to get her to a point where she could stand on her own two feet and take no shit from anyone.

After Hadley left, Holt joined Cayla and Maddie in time for another chapter of *Mr. Popper's Penguins*. Once both dog and child were settled for the night, he and Cayla slipped out of the room. She started to head for the kitchen, but he looped an arm around her waist and steered her into the bedroom, shutting the door behind them and throwing the new lock.

She shot him an arch look. "You know she's going to take longer to go down than that."

"What's wrong?"

Her eyes widened fractionally. "Nothing's wrong."

He closed the distance between them, backing her up against the dresser so he could box her in. "Never play poker. Something's off." Because he couldn't help himself, he brushed the hair back from her face. "Tell me what turned your light down."

After a long, humming beat, she dropped the mask she'd been wearing all night. "Hadley told me about your childhood, your mom. About you." Her eyes were wet as she reached up to frame his face. "No child should have to grow up like that."

She was upset on his behalf. On behalf of the kid he'd never really been. Holt didn't know what to do with that. He'd meant what he'd said to his sister. It was over and done. No reason to get emotional about it now.

Cayla swallowed. "I get why you didn't want to take this on."

Her hands were still on him, but he could feel her pulling back from him.

Desperate to stop it, he wrapped his arms around her, pulling her close. "Don't. Don't judge us based on things I said before I knew you. Yeah, I said that the marriage and family thing was not something I wanted to do. Because I was imagining it would be just another verse of the same song I had growing up. But I was wrong. I hated what I had to do because I was a kid. Because I didn't choose it. I didn't have a partner. I didn't have help. You're nothing like my mother. You're strong and capable, and you would never put anyone ahead of Maddie. I am in this with you a hundred percent. I—" He cut himself off before the rest of that three-word statement could spill out. It still somehow felt too soon. Like it would be pushing. "I *want* to be here, Cayla."

On a sigh, she melted into him, burying her face against his shoulder. "I don't ever want you to feel trapped with us."

"I don't. This marriage is not a cage. It's a home. Maybe the first one I've ever had."

Her head came up, those eyes glistening again. "Holt."

Because those three little words were still fighting to get out, he kissed her instead, drinking deep of the sweetness he couldn't get enough of. She wrapped around him, rising to her toes to press closer. Needing so much more than this, he banded an arm around her and edged backward, toward the oversized chair in the corner. Clearly on the same page, her hands went to his belt, having it undone and his fly down by the time his calves bumped the chair. She shoved his pants down just far enough to free his erection and nudged him to sit, only breaking the kiss long enough to snag a condom from the drawer in the little side table. He didn't know when she'd stashed them there, but he sent up prayers of thanks as she rolled it on. Reaching beneath the skirt of her dress—another piece of forethought he blessed—he tugged down her underwear until she stepped out and crawled into his lap, coming back to take his mouth in a hungry kiss as she sank down, down, down.

They both groaned. She was the first to break the kiss to murmur, "Quiet," against his lips.

He almost laughed. Then she began to move, and all he could focus on was the exquisite torture of her body tight around his. He needed her. Her sweetness. Her light. Her empathy. And he needed this. God, he needed this. For the rest of his natural life. As her muscles began to ripple around him, he made a fresh vow that he'd do anything to protect the peace and the home he'd found with her.

13

T he subtle vibration of Holt's watch had him wide awake in an instant. For a moment, he blinked in the dark before easing his arm from around Cayla so he could read the notification. She murmured in her sleep, shifting to cuddle closer.

When he saw the readout and the follow-up texts, he swore, sitting up and reaching for his prosthesis.

"Holt? What's wrong?" Voice thick with sleep, Cayla pressed a hand to his back. "Did you have a bad dream?"

He wished it were a bad dream. That would be preferable to what he might be walking into. "Alarm's gone off at the bakery. I'm gonna go check it out. Go on back to sleep."

He'd already donned his leg and headed for the closet and the lockbox, where he kept his sidearm by the time she came fully awake and switched on the bedside lamp.

"You shouldn't go up there alone."

"I won't be. The police should already be en route, and the guys are on their way." He checked the magazine and the safety on the Beretta 92FS before sliding it back into the holster and clipping it inside the waistband of his pants.

Cayla's eyes were wide as she tracked the movement.

"It'll be fine. In case you've forgotten, I'm highly trained."

Her cheeks paled. "I also haven't forgotten someone tried to kill Mia up there a few months ago."

"Brax got to him first. I swear, I'll be careful. Try to go back to bed. You need more sleep." He brushed a quick kiss over her temple.

She caught at his hand and squeezed. "There's not a chance in hell I'm going back to sleep. Let me know what's going on as soon as you can."

"Promise."

He pulled out of the driveway just in time to see Brax doing the same from up the street. They made it to the bakery in less than ten minutes. The alarm was still blaring. The cops hadn't arrived yet, but Holt knew from prior experience that Stone County only had two or three deputies on duty at any given time. If they were at the ass end of the county, it might be a while. The vacation rental Jonah had snagged was a bit further out of town as well, so he'd take a few more minutes.

Holt slid out of the 4-Runner as Brax stepped from his truck. Mia sat white-faced in the passenger seat. After what she'd been through here, being held at gunpoint, having a man killed beside her, being here in the middle of the night was hardly going to bring up good memories. But Holt understood why Brax hadn't left her home alone. While he'd shot the man who'd tried to kill her, no one had been able to track down who'd hired the thug.

Brax had his own weapon out. "We waiting on Jonah?"

"Doubt anybody's still inside, but just in case. Split and circle around?"

With a nod, they broke apart, checking the perimeter of the building. The front door remained locked. They'd invested in a heavier door and locking system after events of the spring. But the lock on the rear kitchen door had clearly been jimmied. It hung ajar. Bracing himself for chaos, he nudged the door open and stepped inside for the sweep, Brax on his heels. But the kitchen seemed to be intact. They continued moving through the space, to the swinging door and out to the public area. The front was definitely not fine. But Holt bit back the curse and kept moving until they cleared the bathrooms and confirmed what his gut had already told him. Their perpetrator was long gone.

Holstering his weapon, Holt strode to the security panel and turned off the alarm.

Brax flipped on a light. "Son of a fucking bitch."

The refrigerated bakery cases they'd nabbed for a steal from Nashville had both been overturned, the glass shattered. The floors beneath were likewise damaged, though it wasn't clear whether that was separate or had happened in the course of flipping over the cases.

Jonah strode inside, letting fly a long string of some of the more creative curses Holt had heard during his military career. "One day. We've been open one fucking day for real, and now this?" He paced the room, hands laced behind his head, his boots crunching on pieces of glass.

"I thought we were done with this shit," Brax muttered. "Why now? What purpose does this serve? Mia's not even been on site since the renovation finished over a month ago, other than to pick up food."

Holt stared at the damaged cases. "I don't think this has anything to do with Mia."

"What are you thinking? If it's anything that's gonna put my wife more at ease, I'm game to hear it."

"This feels petty. Vindictive. A strike at *us,* not her." He considered. "What if we were wrong about everything that went down before? What if it had nothing to do with Mia at all?"

"I'm sorry. Did you forget that asshole tried to kill my wife?"

"No, I'm not disputing that. But what if she was just in the wrong place at the wrong time? Everything we found was centered around this place," Holt argued. "When he had Mia, Abruzzi kept talking about a flash drive. Somebody hired him to find some kind of information that he, for whatever reason, believed was here. Think about it. The supply theft slowed down renovations. The vandalism slowed down renovations."

"What about the surveillance equipment in Mia's office?" Brax demanded.

"We didn't find jack shit when we searched her house. The malware Cash found on the Mountainview Construction computers would've given Abruzzi access to work schedules, which would have theoretically given him an idea of when he could search. The surveillance equipment here could have been an effort to keep up with whether that flash drive, or whatever it was he really wanted, was found by one of us or the crew."

Jonah crossed his arms. "You're suggesting that whoever hired Abruzzi hired someone else to pick up where he left off?"

"It's a theory. We never got any true confirmation that everything centered on Mia at all. The evidence was circumstantial. The idea that someone would really come after her ten years after her father's death never sat well with me, but we didn't have any other explanations at the time. Brax had just found out about her past, so it was fresh in his mind, and we didn't have any reason not to go along with it. What if we built the entire theory around confirmation bias?"

Brax stared at him. "Let me get this straight. You think Mia was never in direct danger except for the fact that she was in the wrong place at the wrong time that last night Abruzzi showed up?"

"Maybe." Holt gestured at the busted display cases. "It doesn't make logical sense that this would have anything to do with her. And what are the chances that we'd just happen to get targeted again by someone else mere months later?"

"I mean, I'd love to jump all over that theory because it would mean Mia's safe. But I'm not willing to take any chances with her."

Jonah's brows drew together. "It's a theory worth some consideration. But to play devil's advocate, what if this isn't a strike at us but is actually a strike at *you?* I mean, this wasn't the slick security override we saw before. It was a basic jimmied lock and smash up job. I'm not buying that somebody hired a guy like Abruzzi and then sent a thug with no skills to finish the job. We have to consider that you have Cayla's ex all pissed off that you're in what he considers his territory."

"Is this the kind of thing he'd pull, though?" Brax asked. "He went away for white collar crime, right? Busting shit up doesn't seem to fit."

"I don't know. I'll have to ask her. Right now, I guess we can be grateful that whoever it was didn't get very far into the process. The alarm did its job."

"And so did the cameras. Look."

They all crowded around Jonah's phone to watch the video feed of the break-in. The perpetrator was dressed all in black, including a ski mask. It was hard to tell, but the build seemed right for Raynor. Then again, the guy was pretty average, so the same could be said of a lot of people. Whoever it was came straight in and tipped over the cases, squatting down to do something behind them.

"What's he doing?" Jonah asked.

"Prying up the floorboards. Doesn't know there's concrete underneath, I guess," Brax said.

The sound of tires crunching on gravel drew their attention out front.

"That'll be cops. I'll go meet with the deputy," Jonah sighed.

"I'm gonna go reassure my wife."

As Brax strode out, Holt pulled out his phone to do the same. He opted for a text in case she actually had gone back to sleep.

Had a little break-in. Some vandalism. Everybody's fine.

The phone in his hand vibrated with an incoming call almost immediately. Definitely not asleep.

"Hey."

"How bad?" Cayla asked.

"Not near as bad as what we dealt with before. Alarm scared him off before he could get too far. The bakery cases are toast, but nothing much else seems damaged. There are far more expensive things they could've targeted." He strode back into the kitchen and flipped on the lights to make sure he wasn't a liar. But everything was as spotless and ruthlessly organized as they'd left it. Same with the walk-in cooler.

"That's something, I guess."

"I have to ask, because the cops will. Is this the sort of thing you think Arthur might pull?"

She hesitated. "I wouldn't have thought so. This isn't the sort of thing he's done before. He's not one for getting his hands dirty directly. But maybe? With our credit locked down, he can't get at us via his usual means. And maybe he couldn't find an attorney who'd take a custody case seriously."

Holt very much doubted that was accurate, but his priority at the moment was keeping her calm and making sure she didn't fall into an unnecessary spiral of anxiety.

"Look, the cops are here. We're gonna give our statements and hang around to clean this mess up, figure out what we can do in the meantime so we can still open for business tomorrow." He checked his watch and grimaced. "Today. I'll be in touch later."

"Okay."

"And *try* to go back to bed. I know your day's pretty packed with everything you shifted around to be here for us yesterday."

She sighed. "You're not wrong. I'll make a cup of Sleepytime tea and try to lie back down. I've got Maddie this morning, and if you need to be free to deal with stuff at the bakery in the afternoon, Mama can get her from school."

"I don't know how the day's going to go, so let's just plan on that."

"I'll see you later."

As soon as he'd finished the call with his wife, he dialed another familiar number.

"Dude, do you have any idea what time it is?" Cash complained.

"I do, and I'll consider it payback for you running your mouth and getting me in trouble with my sister."

There was a beat of silence, then the sound of covers rustling. "What do you need?"

CAYLA WAS grateful she'd already planned to clear the morning to work on her office. She understood how the gossip train ran in this town. If she'd had client meetings, talk would inevitably have turned to the latest break-in at the bakery, and people would want answers she didn't have. She didn't know who would spill the beans, but someone would. Likely customers who showed up to find the bakery closed for the day. Holt hadn't been home since he left in the wee hours. He and the guys were hard at work on cleanup and repairs and whatever else was necessary to get them back to business as usual. Not that there'd been time to even establish a usual yet.

One thing she and Holt hadn't discussed in terms of their marriage was finances. It hadn't seemed necessary when they both thought it would be a temporary situation. But as it seemed like maybe it was building toward something more permanent, that meant problems with his business could ultimately impact their household, so she felt compelled to do what was necessary to keep hers in the black. That included making her office a warm, welcoming space for clients. She understood that comfortable clients were more likely to book her services. Plus, having real, professional office space made her look more legit.

The scarred wood floors hadn't been refinished. That was more expense than she wanted for a space she didn't technically own. But she'd found a nice carpet remnant from a flooring retailer in Johnson City and had it bound into a rug that covered most of the surface. Courtesy of Holt, she'd been able to refinish her flea-market sideboard. Redone in the same rustic chic farmhouse style as the dining set she'd repainted— because it was a finish that hid a multitude of blemishes—it now graced the entryway, just waiting for art and accessories to make it pop. The table and chairs had been placed in front of the biggest window. The giant marker board she wanted to hang on the adjacent wall was leaning against it, waiting for another set of hands to help complete the task.

Mia was supposed to stop by for that, but after last night, it was entirely possible she had other things to deal with. Another break-in probably brought up all kinds of terrible memories from what had happened there before. She hadn't talked much about it with Cayla, but it didn't take a genius to see she'd struggled a lot after. Who wouldn't after being held at gunpoint? Thank God for Brax. He'd been Mia's rock through all of it, and seeing the two of them rekindle their marriage after a decade of estrangement had done Cayla's romantic heart good, even before they'd asked her to coordinate their vow renewal ceremony.

Assuming she'd be on her own, Cayla threw herself into finishing what she could without an extra set of hands. Needing the distraction from her own worry, she brought in an array of fun and funky containers she'd picked up for a song at that same flea market. Some would ultimately be repurposed to hold plants. Others would be used for office supplies or to hold business cards and fliers. Still others would be eventually clustered on shelves as examples of the sorts of containers that could be utilized for centerpieces. She'd do a rotation of those on the table from week to week, coordinating with Misty as cross advertising between their businesses. Art came next. Several months back, she'd hit upon a treasure trove of vintage women's magazines from the 1940s. She'd pulled bridal advertisements from all of them and dressed them up with simple mats and black frames. They were unique and, she hoped, classy. She'd just hung the last of them in a grouping on the entryway wall when Mia strode through the door.

"Sorry I'm late. I was helping the guys repair the floor."

"It's totally fine. I kind of figured we'd need to reschedule with everything going on." And given the shadows beneath her eyes, Cayla wasn't entirely sure they shouldn't.

Mia twitched her shoulders, shifting on her feet in a way Cayla recognized as a need to take control of something. "I said I would, and I need to keep busy. I'm too distracted to be on any of my formal job sites today."

"Have they found out anything else since last night?"

She set her toolbox and drill case on the table. "Not really. The police dusted for prints, but there are prints everywhere. It's a public space, and half the town went through there yesterday. Nobody expects them to get very far with that. Meanwhile, the guys have gotten the mess cleaned up and are working on coming up with some kind of alternative display until they can make arrangements to replace the cases."

Cayla winced. "How bad was it? I haven't been over to see for myself. I felt like I might be in the way."

"Once the mess was cleaned up, not terrible. It looked worse than it was last night."

"You were there with the guys last night?"

"Yeah." Mia flipped open the toolbox and pulled out a tape measure, automatically moving to the wall for the marker board.

"That had to be hard after... what happened."

"It wasn't great. But it was better than being left at home to wait and worry."

"I hear that. Obviously, I stayed home with Maddie. Holt kept telling me I should go back to sleep. As if I actually could. So I took advantage of being awake and worked on plans for decorating this place."

Mia scanned what she'd done with the space and nodded. "It's coming together. Gonna look good when you're done. How high do you want this thing?"

Between the two of them, they lifted the marker board, and Mia marked the height.

"Did the guys have any theories about who might have done this?"

She selected a drill bit and popped it in the chuck. "I'd heard your ex was being considered for this. Do you buy that?"

"Holt asked me about that last night. I mean, I have a hard time imagining Arthur doing something like this. It's not his style. He's all about trying to outsmart people because he likes to believe that he's the smartest person in the room. This feels too... brutish? Which isn't to say he doesn't have a temper or the capacity to destroy things. He certainly looked pissed off enough when he left here and might want to do something to Holt. Although if this was about Holt and making the business fail, why not attack the ovens and equipment? The stuff they have to have to run the bakery? I mean, losing the refrigerated cases isn't great, but they can work around that."

"Fair point." Mia drilled the pilot holes. "How is that whole situation, anyway?"

"Quiet. Too quiet. When Arthur showed up here, I was terrified. He made threats, and I was so scared and so sure he was really going to cause problems that I actually agreed to Holt's lunatic plan of getting married. But other than one attempt to open a credit account in my name—which I can't actually prove was him. I only suspect because of the timing—he hasn't done anything. It's been nearly a month, and it's making me twitchy. He's not a man who makes idle threats."

Humming a noncommittal noise, Mia pounded in the wall anchors before turning to face her. "This is not really my business, but I'm gonna ask anyway. Feel free not to answer."

Cayla tensed, wondering where she was going with this. "Okay."

"Are you regretting marrying Holt?"

She relaxed again. "No. He's wonderful. He's great with Maddie, great with me. He feels like a frickin' unicorn. This perfect guy who's suddenly in my life."

"And your bed?"

Cayla tipped her head in acknowledgement. "You know I've wanted him for a long time. Being consenting *married* adults, it seems like that was an inevitability. Definitely no regrets there."

Mia studied her. "I sense a 'but'."

Was it fair to get into the 'but' when Holt had been trying so hard to reassure her? She'd felt better in the moment. Always better when she was with him. But when they were apart, the doubts always seemed to creep back in. Maybe it would help to discuss it with another woman.

"I've had concerns because, with his background, taking on an instant family was not something he wanted to do. It was the primary reason he didn't pursue me before. We've talked about it, and he says he was wrong about that, and he wants to be here. I know he believes that, and I do believe there's definitely something between us."

That something was very much love on her side. But how could she say anything to Mia about it? If it got back to Brax, it might get to Holt. He needed to be the one to hear it first, and she wasn't ready for that step.

They lapsed into silence as they wrestled the marker board into place, and Mia put in the screws. As she stepped down from the stool, she set the drill aside. "You went into this marriage to him with an idea that it was temporary. Are you thinking now that maybe it won't be?"

"I don't know what it'll be. I know what we have is good. I know we're building something. And I know I don't want to let that something go. But I just don't think we can really trust whatever is between us until the situation with Arthur is resolved. Because I'll always have that question in the back of my mind of whether that's the only reason he's still here."

"Makes sense. It's a reasonable concern. He's a caretaking kind of guy. If it makes you feel any better, by all observations from the rest of us, he adores you both. He's happier, more relaxed. Easier than when he first got to town. I think you're good for him. I think the family life is good for him."

It made her feel better to hear it from people who knew him better than she did. "I know he's good for us." She bit her lip. "Is that crazy? The idea that we jumped into this—not exactly on a whim, but under duress—and it's actually... right?"

"Crazier things have happened. Brax and I certainly didn't have a traditional courtship. Hell, we didn't even date before we got married. Not until we'd been estranged for ten years and came back together here. So I'm the last person to say that there is a single path to love and happiness. As far as I'm concerned, if you two make each other happy, then do whatever you have to in order to protect it."

That was exactly what Cayla planned to do.

14

It took longer than Holt wanted to get his sister on her way. In all the chaos, he'd entirely forgotten she was stopping by. By the time he'd answered her myriad questions —mostly with a lot of "We don't know"—Mia had finished repairs on the floor.

"Seriously, Had, I've got to deal with this."

"Fine. I'll get out of your hair, if only because I need to get back to Knoxville to catch my flight."

He walked her out to her rental car, wishing things weren't such a mess and that he had more time to spend with her. "Text me when you get home, okay?"

"Yes, Dad." Hadley rolled her eyes but grabbed him in a hug. "And hey, I really hope I didn't accidentally muck things up for you with Cayla yesterday. I think she's perfect for you."

It meant something to have his sister's approval, even if he hadn't asked for it. Maybe, on some level, that had also been part of why he hadn't told Hadley about his precipitous marriage. Because he knew she needed it, he found the ghost of a smile. "I think we're sorted. Thanks."

She slid into the driver's seat. "Love you, Jerkface."

"Love you back, Squirt."

He stood for a moment, watching her drive away. His gaze automatically shifted across the street. Mia's truck was parked beside Cayla's car. Good. Hopefully, they'd both stay occupied enough finishing up her office and not worry about the situation over here.

Jonah stood over Brax's shoulder in the tiny office off the kitchen, as they both looked at the computer.

Holt leaned in the doorway. "Well?"

"I have scoured the internet, including that used restaurant supply site where we found that awesome deal on the original cases, but there ain't jack to be had right now. Replacements are going to run in the several thousand dollar range."

"Not good." Shifting on his feet, Holt rubbed at his bad knee. "I mean, we can make a claim on our insurance, but how's it going to look to be doing that straight out of the gate? What kind of rate increase might we expect over the long-term if we do that?"

Jonah straightened, folding his arms. "I mean, technically, if we all pool our funds, we can pull off buying new ones outright."

Brax twisted around to look at them both. "True, but I've got some financial responsibilities I didn't have when I signed on for this. It's only right that I contribute to the cost of the home renovations with Mia. I already put as much as I was comfortable putting in on the front end so we wouldn't have to take out lines of credit to pay for construction and startup."

"And I've got a responsibility to keep a cushion in savings for my family." The words slipped out before Holt could think better of them. When the hell had he started thinking in those terms?

His friends both went brows up.

"So, it's getting serious." Jonah didn't phrase it as a question.

What was the point of pussyfooting around it? "Yeah. Yeah, I think it is."

"Good for you, brother," Brax declared.

Holt moved aside so they could come out of the office.

Jonah clapped him on the shoulder as he passed. "Yeah. We're happy for you, man. And it's totally fine. We went through this whole process without taking out any business loans. This would be a small one, in the grand scheme of things. We'll go on down to the bank. It shouldn't be that big a deal."

As there was no time like the present, they loaded up in Jonah's truck and headed downtown. They strode in as a unit. Naturally, Jonah knew half the people there. Holt stood back while he did the glad-handing that seemed to go along with small-town life. A few minutes later, a customer service rep led them back to an office. Because his knee was aching, he took one of the two chairs available. Jonah took the other, and Brax stood sentry behind them.

The CSR folded her hands and offered a smile. "Now, what can I do for you, gentlemen?"

As the resident hometown boy, Jonah took point. "We're looking at a small business loan. We had some vandalism up at our place last night and need to replace some equipment." He told her the amount they were looking for.

"All right. I'll just need to get some information from the three of you." One by one, they provided the details requested. The woman's fingers flew over the keyboard, filling out the requisite paperwork. She finished with an enthusiastic keystroke. "There now. Let's see what kind of rates the system spits back out."

The desktop computer made a humming noise.

"This old thing's a little slow." She flashed another smile and turned back to the screen.

Holt knew something was wrong immediately. Her lips

pressed together, and her brows pulled down. A few more clicks to confirm whatever she'd found, and she turned back to them, folding her hands with the finality of shutting a door.

"I'm afraid the bank won't be able to extend you that line of credit." The tone and expression were apologetic.

Jonah, ever affable, just arched a brow. "What's the problem?"

She hesitated. "Well, your credit scores aren't high enough, and there are some concerning patterns in your credit reports."

Holt's gut twisted.

"Concerning patterns?" Brax asked. "We haven't been using credit at all for this business, and for the most part, we were all out of the country deployed for years before that."

The woman's expression turned sympathetic. "Y'all all may want to pull your credit reports and make sure you haven't been victims of fraud."

Fraud. Identity theft.

The three of them exchanged a look. Petty vandalism might not be like Raynor, but this was exactly the shit he'd gone to prison for.

Knowing it wouldn't get dealt with here, they all rose without a fuss, thanked the woman, and left the bank.

Nobody said anything until they got in the truck.

Brax leaned forward, bracing his arms on the front seats. "This sounds bad."

"No reason to panic until we have all the intel," Jonah insisted. "We'll head to my place. We won't get interrupted there."

Half an hour later, they were all poring over copies of their respective credit reports. Reports that told a damning story. Multiple accounts had been opened for all of them. Nearly a hundred grand of debt had already been run up in mere weeks across the three of them.

Holt shook his head. "I don't understand. As soon as Cayla

told me, I locked my credit down. I didn't think to mention it to you two at the time because there was no reason to think he'd be coming after you. But this shouldn't be possible."

Brax tossed his report onto the coffee table. "Well, looks like it is. And looks like Raynor's got more balls than we gave him credit for. We do take this as confirmation that it's him, right?"

"Has to be. Cayla said he had skills." So much for his earlier theory. Scrubbing both hands over his face, Holt swore. "I've been telling her we'd be fine. That we were being careful. Vigilant. But clearly I missed something. And now you two have been dragged into all this because of me." Guilt weighed heavy on his shoulders. He'd gotten into this to protect her and now his friends and prospectively his business were getting dragged down with him.

"Recriminations aren't going to help a damned thing," Jonah pointed out. "So, what are we gonna do?"

Holt blew out a breath. "What we're not gonna do is tell my wife. Not yet. If she sees this level of damage, she's going to freak out, and she's already worried enough. So right now, let's get the ball rolling, report fraud on all these false accounts. We'll contact Cash, get him to do whatever he can do. Get any information he can that will aid our cause. It's gonna take time to unravel. I want to know what we're doing about it before I tell her what's happening."

Jonah nodded. "Makes sense."

Brax looked skeptical. "I get where you're coming from, but is that the best course of action?"

"What's an extra day gonna hurt? We can take one day and figure our shit out, so when I tell her, a plan will already be in place. I'll tell her tomorrow."

He just hoped he had more positive news to share when he did.

∾

"You heard about the break-in up at Bad Boy Bakers, didn't you?"

Cayla's hands tightened on the cart handle as she made her way through Garden of Eden for her weekly grocery run.

"No! What happened?"

"Another middle-of-the-night break-in. Smashed the front all to pieces, I heard."

"Those poor boys. They've been working so hard to make a go of it."

"You really have to wonder if the location's cursed. I mean, given the questionable clientele The Right Attitude used to have."

"That's just silly. Why would any of that have anything to do with them? They're good boys and the bakery is a wonderful addition to the Eden's Ridge. Have you tried their coffeecake.? It is *to die for*."

In the two days since the break-in, Cayla had been hearing more of the same all over town. Everybody was abuzz, and in the absence of factual information, people were plenty happy to manufacture some. Not wanting to engage, she kept her head down and finished up her shopping.

From behind the register, Ina Hanes flashed her a sympathetic smile as she began loading her items onto the belt. "Hey, Cayla."

"Ina."

"How's that sweet girl of yours?"

"Growing like a weed and counting the days until summer vacation."

"That's always the way. What about that handsome hubby of yours? I heard they had a spot of trouble up at the bakery."

Knowing better than to feed the gossip beast, Cayla just smiled. "Nothing they can't handle. Did you know Marisol Sanz just got engaged to Shayne McDermott?"

Ina took the conversational bone and ran with it. "I did. I heard all about it from Peggy Wheaton."

Cayla made it out of the grocery store with the full account of the proposal and a plan to check in with Marisol next week to see if she'd begun thinking about engagement parties or the wedding itself. She just needed to swing by the bank before heading home to drop these groceries.

The lobby was mostly empty this time of day. Too late for lunch, too early for the after-school crowd. She stopped by the counter in the middle of the lobby and began to fill out a deposit slip.

"Hey, Cayla!"

She looked up to find Brandy Brighton, one of the customer service representatives, whom she'd gone to high school with what felt like a hundred years ago. "Hey Brandy."

"I just wanted to pop over and say again how much my sister enjoyed that baby shower you organized back in the spring."

"It was my pleasure. Babies are such blessings."

"Aren't they, though? And my new nephew is just the cutest thing ever." She promptly pulled out her phone and flashed pictures of the newborn.

Cayla made the appropriate noises of admiration and finished filling out her deposit slip.

"Anyway, I was really sorry the bank wasn't able to extend a line of credit to the guys to help—you know—make up for things after this latest... unpleasantness."

"I'm sorry?"

Brandy's round cheeks pinked as she realized Cayla had no idea what she was talking about. "I... oh. I misspoke."

"I don't think you did. My husband and his partners were in here for a line of credit?"

"I, um, think that's something you'll need to discuss with

your husband." She began backing away. "It was good to see you."

Holt had said nothing about going to the bank. Nothing about needing a line of credit to replace the cases destroyed at the bakery. She'd assumed insurance would cover it. Which meant he was keeping things from her. It wasn't the same as with Arthur. She knew that. She knew Holt wasn't that kind of man. But it didn't stop the sick, oily feeling from churning in her gut. She was willing to put up with him not sharing a lot about his past, understanding that kind of trust would take time to build. But she sure as hell wouldn't stand for being kept in the dark about something that was clearly related to the threat they were supposed to be facing together.

Stuffing the deposit slip into her purse, she marched out of the bank and drove straight to the bakery. He was serving a customer when she came in and offered her a little smile and a wave. Temper still simmering, she hung back by the door, taking in the temporary displays they'd arranged in baskets on a few card tables until they got new refrigerated cases. Beyond the pass-thru, she spotted Jonah and Brax working. Good. She wanted to talk to them, too.

As soon as the customer departed, she flipped the sign from open to closed and locked the door.

Holt was around the counter in a flash, brow creased with concern. "What's wrong? What happened?"

Not bothering to hide the temper, she stepped around him before he could touch her and shoved her way into the kitchen. Brax and Jonah looked up in surprise.

She divided a narrow-eyed gaze between them all. "Do y'all have something you want to tell me?"

Jonah and Brax looked at each other and pointed directly at Holt.

"What's the matter?" he demanded.

She propped her fists on her hips and glared at him. "I just ran into Brandy Brighton at the bank, who tells me that, for whatever reason, they couldn't extend y'all a line of credit for what shouldn't amount to that much of a business loan to deal with the new bakery cases."

Though his expression didn't change, he shifted on his feet, a sure sign he was uncomfortable. "Yeah."

"Have y'all all checked your credit reports?"

Again, Brax and Jonah looked at Holt.

She infused her voice with every ounce of mom-guilt she could muster. "Don't you look at him. You look at me."

As their expressions shifted to guilty, she shook her head. "He's gotten to you. He's gotten to all three of you, hasn't he?" The sick churn turned into full on knots as she realized that everything she'd imagined on the drive over here was probably only the tip of the iceberg.

Holt stepped toward her. "Cayla, honey, we're handling it."

"You're handling it? You're handling it. By keeping me in the dark? That's not acceptable. Not now, not ever. Not to me."

Regret flashed over his face. "Look, I'm sorry, but I didn't want to worry you until I had more information—"

She held up a hand and struggled to modulate her voice. "No. We are not doing that shit. Information is power, and I will not be cut out. Not for what you perceive to be my own good. Not for any reason. I am too far down this path with you. I won't live like that again. Right now, I'm calling my contact with the FBI, and all three of you are going to give him whatever information you have, because it is very clear that my ex-husband is up to his old tricks, and he's not satisfied with trying to just ruin me." She rounded on Holt. "Then *we* are going home to have a conversation about this."

As her phone vibrated with a reminder of her upcoming meeting, she blew out a breath through her nose. "Scratch that. You're talking to Special Agent Marquez, and then I'm going back to work. After which, I will see you at home, and we are having that conversation."

With shaking hands, she jabbed at the buttons on her phone, putting through the call to her contact. Thank God he'd given her his direct cell number.

"Ms. Black, is everything all right?"

"That is a decided, 'no'. My ex-husband is up to his old tricks again. I have three people that you need to talk to. Hopefully, they'll be able to give you enough to continue building a fresh case against him."

With a fulminating look, she handed the phone to her husband and leaned back to listen.

15

Holt stepped out of Moonbeams and Sweet Dreams, an enormous bouquet in hand and a glare of judgment at his back from its quiet proprietress. Misty hadn't let on that she knew what was going on, but he supposed it was obvious enough he was in the doghouse and angling to get out of it. Girl Code probably dictated she be on Cayla's side, regardless. He could respect the support, but he was damned glad he hadn't been treated to a tongue-lashing from her, too. The one he'd gotten from his wife had been bad enough.

In his time with her, Holt had seen Cayla all different shades of happy. The happy was what had drawn him in, despite himself. It was the terrified fragility that had pulled at him, overcoming his initial reservations to land him a front-row seat to her life. Since then, he'd been witness to passion, exhaustion, frustration, and the edge of a total overwhelmed meltdown. But he'd never seen her angry. He hadn't imagined she had that level of fury in her and was more than a little shamed that it had been directed at him. In front of his friends. Hell, they'd been thoroughly chastened, too. The shame pissed him off. He'd been doing what he believed was right in the name of protecting her. That should damned well count for something.

"You're scowling awfully hard at those flowers."

He looked up to find Rebecca smiling at him. "Hey. What are you doing here?"

"Just finished up with my last client of the day and spotted you down here. Thought I'd come say hello. Where are you off to?"

"Home." Where he'd be having a *conversation*, per Cayla's edict. All the possible negative outcomes of that scenario had his gut tied in knots. Hence the flowers.

She studied him, those green eyes she shared with her son, seeing way too much. "You have the look of a man who's just had a fight with his wife."

"That obvious?"

"I have keen powers of deduction." Her smile softened the sarcasm. Tucking a hand in the crook of his arm, she tugged. "Walk with me."

Holt gave her a little bit of side eye but fell into step beside her. "Is this the part where you mom me?"

Rebecca glanced up at him from beneath those ridiculously long, former pageant queen lashes. "Do you need momming?"

God knew he'd never had it from his own. "Can't hurt. Brax said you give good advice."

"Well, I can try. Why don't you tell me what happened?"

Hell, it couldn't hurt to have the perspective of another woman.

As they strolled along Main Street, down toward the city park, Holt kept his eye out for eavesdroppers and laid it out—leaving out the details about how Brax and Jonah had been involved since that wasn't his to tell. His shoulders had risen toward his ears by the end. "I had good reason for doing it the way I did."

"I'm sure you feel like you did."

His shoulders hunched some more. He hadn't done this to get lambasted by another female in his life. "I was a Ranger. I'm used to giving orders, taking action. Checking in like this, giving partial intel, is not part of my way of operating. It's inefficient. My superior officers expected answers, not half-assed reports."

"I get that. My son's a SEAL, after all, so you're cut from the same cloth. But first off, you need to remember that life is not a mission. You're dealing with civilians, not other trained soldiers. Aside from that, you need to remember that your wife is a partner, not a superior. A partner gets included in things."

"I wasn't excluding her. I was trying to save her from some stress. God knows, she's had enough."

"True, but I still think you should give Cayla some more credit. She's stronger than you realize."

"I never said she wasn't strong or capable." She was one of the most capable people he'd ever known.

"Maybe not with words. But stop and think a minute. How much do you think it took her to go to the FBI about her husband in the first place? How much more do you think it took her to leave him? To divorce him and raise that child on her own?"

"It took an amazing amount of courage, but—"

"I'm not finished."

Her tone was mild, but the rebuke was firm, so Holt shut his mouth.

"She came out of an abusive marriage to an incredibly controlling man who kept major secrets. It damaged her ability to trust. In all the years she's been back, I haven't seen or heard of her even saying yes to dinner with somebody. She hasn't let anybody in until you, and then you turn around and keep something huge from her. That's a really big deal." Rebecca stopped and pulled him down to sit on one of the park benches. "Now, I don't doubt you were well-intentioned. You're a good man, Holt. And maybe you didn't plan to keep it from her forever, like he did. But she didn't know that. How's that gonna feel to her?"

Surely she wasn't equating him to Raynor. The very idea of it put his back up. "I wasn't keeping it from her to hide it. I just wanted the full picture before I brought it to her. It was a *day*."

"That may be, but it still doesn't change the fact that she got blindsided, just like before, so it's bound to be stirring up all those feelings all over again."

Cellophane crinkled as his hand fisted around the flowers. He forced himself to relax. "I'm not him. She can trust me. I'd never do anything to hurt her."

"Not on purpose," Rebecca agreed. "But you two are still new, and you've both got a lot of baggage to work through to understand each other. You would, even if you weren't in this rather unusual situation. So what I'm telling you, son, is to keep that in mind when you go home to talk about this. You deserve the chance to explain yourself, but be sure to actually *listen* when she talks. Don't just wait for a pause in the conversation so you can explain why she's wrong."

He sighed, staring out over the lush expanse of spring green grass. "I was trying to protect her. I didn't want to worry her any more than I already had to because she's already got so much on her. But I can see now that being kept in the dark probably upset her more than the details. I didn't count on someone else telling her before I did."

Rebecca nodded in approval. "Tell her *that*. It acknowledges and validates her perspective, while still getting your reasons in."

He could do that. But as he remembered the twin expressions of hurt and disappointment on her face, he had to acknowledge, "Flowers and an apology don't seem like enough."

She looked at the bouquet he still held. "Oh, yeah. I'd go bigger."

CAYLA WAS ALMOST at the end of her rope. Her client meeting had been a disaster. Her ex-husband had been on a veritable identity theft rampage. And Maddie seemed intent on being her most obstinate, complaining about what was for dinner, about doing homework, about not having more play time with Banana Bread. She'd ended up in tears over being told to get in the bath. Cayla knew her daughter was mostly likely responding to the fact that she herself was keyed up and worried. And that Holt hadn't come home yet.

Cayla had no idea where he was or what he was doing. A man like him probably wouldn't respond well to the ultimatum she'd issued. Maybe she shouldn't have laid into him—into all of them—the way she had. But how foolish could the lot of them be? Very, apparently. After hearing the full scope of what Arthur had managed to do to Holt and his friends, she'd wanted to vomit. This was the sneak attack they hadn't seen coming, and she didn't know whether it could be fixed. There were measures to fight. But it could take years, and who knew if their fledgling business would survive in the meantime? That was on her. They'd all been targeted because of her.

She tugged a pajama top over Maddie's head, pausing to wipe at those tear-stained cheeks. "I'm sorry we're both having bad days, Munchkin. Let's go on to bed. Tomorrow will be better." Cayla suspected it wouldn't, but she'd at least provide some hope for her daughter.

Maddie sniffed. "Where's Daddy?"

Cayla's heart squeezed. Of course she'd be thinking of Holt as her father. He'd been more of one these past weeks than her own ever had. She didn't have the heart to correct Maddie.

The truth was, she had no idea where Holt was. He hadn't texted. She hadn't called to track him down. She wasn't even sure if he'd answer if she did. "He got tied up at the bakery, baby. You'll see him tomorrow."

God, Cayla hoped he didn't make a liar out of her because she'd wounded his pride. She didn't think he was that kind of man, but she hadn't imagined he'd keep something this big from her, either.

That lower lip quivered. "Can I have two chapters tonight?"

It felt like the least she could do. "Yeah. I think we can do that." She crawled into bed beside her daughter.

BB leaped up, turning three circles before flopping onto the end of the bed. Cayla didn't have the heart to send the dog to her crate. She hadn't had an accident in the house, so tonight was as good a test of her house training as any. The three of them settled in to read. Maddie was calmer at the end, her little eyes drooping. Cayla set the book aside and tucked her in, lingering over the bubblegum scent of her shampoo.

Anything. She'd do anything to protect her most precious girl.

"Good night, Munchkin."

"Night, Mommy."

Slipping quietly from the room, she pulled the door almost closed and let out a slow, shuddering breath. She really, really wanted a good cry, but that wasn't an option. Holding her shit together was imperative. Because she always had to hold her shit together. That was the gig.

A sound drew her to the kitchen. On the way, she noted the toys had been cleared. As BB hadn't been taught that trick, Holt must be back. She found him at the sink, finishing the last of the dishes from the dinner he hadn't been here to eat.

He set the pan in the dish drainer and wiped his hands. "Hey."

Relief that he'd come home at all warred with frustration and fear and uncertainty about where they stood. "Hi."

He held out a hand. "Will you come with me?"

Was he kidding right now? "I'm really not in the mood."

"Not for that. I have something I want to show you."

She was beyond exhausted, but she'd demanded a conversation. If that meant going with him, so be it. She didn't take the hand he'd offered. If that hurt or offended him, he didn't show it. He moved past her and opened the door to the backyard. Well out of the hearing of little ears. That didn't bode well. Her stomach cramped, but she followed him out.

"Shouldn't we turn on a light?"

Holt just tapped the screen of his phone. Twinkle lights blinked on. Hundreds of them, wrapped around the big oak tree. From one of the massive branches hung a porch swing that hadn't been there before. Beside it, on a little table she didn't recognize, stood a bottle of wine and a bouquet of flowers.

When had he *done* all this?

He stuffed his hands in his pockets, his big shoulders a little hunched, but he met her gaze head-on. "I owe you an apology. I should have told you yesterday as soon as we found out what had happened. I get that you're upset, but I need you to understand that I didn't keep it from you out of disrespect or an effort to control you. I just wanted to be able to tell you it was being taken care of, so you'd know there was a plan in place and you didn't have to take all that on yourself. Because you will. You did. The moment you found out, you started blaming yourself."

She had. Because none of them would be in this position if not for her. But he didn't seem to be finished.

"I can see where I went wrong in how I approached that. I never wanted you to feel like I thought you weren't strong. I know exactly how strong you are with everything you've done. I know because I did the same for Hadley when we were growing up. I know what it is to have to carry that burden alone and never get a break. To always have to hold everything together."

Was the man a mind reader? It was as if he was responding to everything she'd been thinking but hadn't said tonight. That he saw it, recognized it, had her throat going tight with tears she didn't have the energy to hold back.

"So I put up this swing to remind you that you get to take a break once in a while. Because you're not alone anymore. You have me. And I know things are tough right now, but we're going to find a way out the other side. Because this might be our first fight, but I sure as hell hope it's not our last." He paused, frowned. "That came out wrong."

She laughed a little, wiping at her own cheeks. "I know what you meant." Heaving a heavy sigh, she let go of a little of the fear. "I don't want this to be over either."

He swallowed and nodded, turning to the wine. With his usual efficiency, he pulled the cork and poured a glass. "Sit. We can still hash all this out. But right now, I'm gonna let you have some much needed quiet time to reset."

When he turned to go back inside, she laid a tentative hand on his arm. "You could sit with me."

His strong, callused fingers settled over hers, reforging a connection that had been fractured. "I'd like that."

Gripping her glass, Cayla curled her hand around the chain and sat. Holt eased down beside her, stretching an arm along the back of the swing. She leaned into him, relaxing against his familiar warmth, feeling his arm come around her, so grateful it wasn't the last time.

"I hated today," she murmured.

"So did I."

"I'm sorry I yelled at you. At all of you. I just... I got sucker-punched by the whole thing, and after what I lived through before, I have a hair-trigger response to secrets. Particularly financial secrets."

"I get that. I didn't think of it in the moment, but I get it. I won't do it again."

"Thank you." She angled toward him, sliding a hand along his jaw to tip his face down. He came willingly, his mouth warm against hers. They both sighed into the kiss, the last of the roughness between them smoothing out. Why couldn't everything be as simple as this feeling of rightness?

With one last sip of him, she eased back, settling into the comfortable curve of his arm. He nudged the swing into motion, and they sat in companionable silence, watching the fireflies dance.

Eventually, Cayla's curiosity overrode her need for silence. "What exactly are you doing to handle the situation?"

"We've all made the requisite reports to the FTC and all the credit bureaus about the false accounts. And Cash is looking into things. Unless Arthur somehow became a hacker in prison, he didn't get into my shit on his own. I locked it down as soon as you said I should."

Her warning hadn't been enough. How were they supposed to combat that?

With a heavy sigh, she sipped more wine. "I didn't think to warn Brax and Jonah. It never occurred to me he might go after them. It should have. They're your business partners. It makes a sick sort of sense that he'd target all of you."

"It didn't occur to me either. And, yeah, it's not great. But let me be clear, they're not pissed at you. You didn't do this."

"Not directly, but it doesn't change the fact that none of you would be in this situation if not for me."

"Don't." Holt squeezed her shoulder. "You can't blame yourself. He wants you to do that. It's more manipulation on his part. This shit is a pain in the ass, but it's not impossible to reverse. We *will* get it sorted."

She wondered if he'd learned this unwavering confidence as a Ranger or if he'd always been like this. Either way, she appreciated the support. They didn't have answers yet. In all likelihood, Arthur's campaign was just beginning. That prospect was terrifying. She didn't know what he'd do next.

But she and Holt had each other. That was enough for now.

16

T en days. A week and a half without answers. Without action.

Holt was beyond twitchy. He knew how to wait. How to hold out for the right moment to execute a directive. But this wasn't the sort of fight he'd been trained for. He didn't have the computer or investigative skills necessary to undo the damage that had been done. So he had to rely on others. Some, like Cash, he trusted. Others, like the FBI agents allegedly working to prove Raynor's current felonious activity, in addition to shoring up whatever weaknesses existed in the original case, he didn't. Oh, he was sure they were doing their jobs. But it wasn't their families, their livelihoods on the line, so they weren't motivated in the same way. Holt needed to put an end to this. And while he knew countless ways to track down and neutralize the threat Raynor posed, he was a civilian now, without orders or just cause for taking a life.

So he waited, filling his days with flour, sugar, and butter in the exacting, methodical fashion that had come to soothe him during his tenure in Dr. Graham's program. Baking was a thing he could control, with results he could predict. And it was the only way they were going to keep their business afloat.

Customers were coming. Not in the droves of the very beginning, but steady enough. There'd been plenty of Looky Lous fishing for information about the break-in. They were sticking with the party line that the vandal hadn't been caught, and the police were looking into it. So far, nobody had been brave enough to ask or opine to their faces about any connection to the trouble they'd had during the renovation.

Without the refrigerated display cases, he and his partners had switched to baking things more in shifts rather than prepping the whole day's wares at once. Since the bulk of his contribution to the bottom line were the custom cakes he had, thankfully, gotten a steady stream of orders for, he came in later, which meant he was around for the morning routine at home, getting Maddie off to school. That part of the change he liked, and not just because he felt like she was better protected if he saw her to and from the elementary school.

For her part, Cayla had taken to working out front in the bakery, both for planning and client meetings, when she could arrange it. She didn't like it, not when she'd only just gotten her office ready for clients. But Holt hadn't forgotten how Raynor had cornered her there, and he didn't want to give the slimeball a chance to do it again. Here she was protected, both by dint of being in public and by always being within shouting distance of the three of them. And he had to admit, he enjoyed being able to glance through the pass-thru and see her tapping away on her tidy little laptop or making notes in the composition books she preferred at one of the four-top tables.

This morning she sat with the newly engaged Marisol Sanz, discussing options for an engagement party. It amazed him how easily she could just reach out to strangers to offer her services. She came off as the well-organized friend who just wanted to take something off their plates and make life easier, which was, he'd decided, the secret to her success. Marisol fairly glowed with happiness, her hands waving as she talked with apparent enthusiasm over whatever Cayla had suggested.

The door opened, and another customer came in. Holt pegged the guy in his late twenties. He wore jeans and an untucked Oxford cloth shirt, with the sleeves rolled to his elbows. One hand curled around the strap of a messenger bag hung over across his narrow chest. The heavy-framed black glasses gave him a vaguely Clark Kent vibe, though he was too wiry to fool anyone into thinking he was Superman. He glanced around the bakery before stepping up to their new counter. Mia had improvised a clever display out of reclaimed wood and old windows. It wasn't refrigerated, but it did the trick of displaying their wares in a more professional fashion than the card tables and baskets they'd been working with, and the price tag had been minimal, which was a concern these days.

Because it was his turn, Holt pushed past the swinging door to go out front. "Help you?"

"Yeah, can I get one of those apple cinnamon scones?"

"Sure. For here or to go?"

"To go, please."

Holt opened the door on the back of the case and reached in with a square of parchment paper to grab a scone off the end of the tray closest to him. "You want this heated?"

"Nah, I'm good. Thanks."

Holt bagged the scone and rang the guy up, accepting the cash payment and making change. "Have a good one."

"Thanks, man." The guy stuffed his change into his pocket and opened the messenger bag to put his purchase inside. As he turned, his eyes landed on Cayla and brightened with recognition.

Someone else she'd gone to high school with? The age was about right. Holt watched as the guy strode over to her table.

"Cayla Black, right?"

She looked up, confusion flickering over her face. The lack of recognition on her side had some instinctive alarm sounding, and Holt was already moving out from behind the counter as she said, "Yes?"

He dropped an envelope on her laptop. "You've been served."

Holt growled, his hands curling into fists.

The Clark Kent wannabe took two stumbling steps back, face paling as he caught sight of Holt. "Just doing my job, man."

"Get out."

He booked it out of the bakery. Cayla looked at the door, at Holt, and then finally down at the envelope as if it were a snake about to strike. She'd gone sheet white. Because this was the thing they'd been waiting for. This was what they'd been expecting for weeks. It had to be.

Marisol looked acutely uncomfortable. "I think we've got enough for now. I'll talk everything over with Shayne and be in touch."

Cayla worked up a smile, though it was brittle around the edges. "Great. And I apologize for the interruption."

As soon as the girl left, Holt locked the door behind her. Brax and Jonah came out from the kitchen, hovering near the counter. Holt sat down across from Cayla, who was still staring at the envelope.

He kept his voice gentle, understanding her fear. "Do you want me to open it?"

She shook her head, reaching for it with trembling fingers. Ripping it open, she slid out the contents and unfolded them. As her eyes read over the paperwork, her face paled further. Without a word, she handed it to him.

Holt skimmed it, not absorbing the details beyond the fact that Raynor was suing for full custody of Maddie. Struggling not to crush the petition in his hand, he set it aside and reached for his wife. Her fingers felt icy in his.

"We knew this was probably coming. He let us get complacent. It's why he waited. To have maximum impact and upset you more. It's gonna be okay. Another pain in the ass, but we're going to get through it."

Some alert sounded on her phone. She picked it up to check. At the sight of the notification, she went almost gray. Yanking her hand from his, she fumbled with the screen, opening some app and scrolling through, clearly checking several things.

"What is it?"

She closed her eyes, tears leaking out as she struggled to speak. "The identity theft protection service I use. He's cracked my and Maddie's identities and done the same damned thing to both of us."

"I swear to you, we're doing everything we can to get to the bottom of this," Special Agent Marquez insisted.

Cayla bit back the bitter laugh that wanted to spill out. "I came to you six years ago because I believed you'd be able to see that he was stopped and punished for all the people he'd hurt. You assured me you would. Yet here we are, with him out of the cage on some kind of technicality, free to go back to exactly what he was doing before. Except instead of strangers, he's doing it to me. To my husband. To my friends. You'll have to forgive me if I don't think your best is currently good enough."

Was her accusation harsh and unfair? Maybe. But she was beyond giving a damn. The past couple of weeks had shown her exactly how poor the protections she'd put into place really were. Arthur might not be able to lay hands on her physically, thanks to Holt, but he could get to her every other way. And she knew he'd continue to prove it until someone stopped him.

Special Agent Marquez sighed. "I know this really means nothing, under the circumstances, but I really am sorry. I wish things were moving quicker. But we're trying to be thorough. To make sure we don't have a repeat of this appeal when we put him away again. And we *will* put him away again. We just need time."

"Unfortunately, that's something we may not have. Please keep me informed."

After listening to his empty assurances, Cayla hung up and dropped her face into her hands. She'd known before she called him that the FBI wouldn't be able to *do* anything. But she'd reported the details, exactly as she'd promised. She'd contacted the FTC and the credit bureaus, starting the same process Holt and the guys had already begun. What more could they do? They were meeting with an attorney in Johnson City tomorrow to go over the petition and formulate a response. That was the next logical step. But financially? She didn't know how they were going to weather this.

She'd dipped into savings to finish outfitting her office as a business growth tactic. Certainly, she had business coming in— thank God—but would it be enough to cover them with the bakery being in a precarious financial position itself? In all reality, Arthur had financially hobbled them. They could limp along for a while longer, but if anything else happened, they'd be completely screwed. Not to mention the question of how they were going to afford the attorney if the custody suit had any real grounds.

From the living room, she could hear the low rumble of Holt's voice. He'd been on the phone with Cash for the last twenty minutes going over the latest. She wasn't exactly clear on what it was Cash was doing, but Holt had let slip that he was former Army Intelligence, so maybe he had some skills or access to information the FBI couldn't tap. At this point, she didn't care who put Arthur behind bars again, only that they do it soon.

Her phone rang. Unknown number.

With a sense of foreboding, she hit answer. "Hello."

"Hello, Cayla." Arthur's familiar, supercilious voice sent a chill down her spine.

"What do you want?"

"I only want what's mine. Nothing more. Nothing less."

"And what exactly do you consider yours?" She knew, but this was how the game was played.

"Well, you've gotten the custody paperwork by now."

Her hand curled tight around the edge of the table, knuckles going white. "Yes."

"Your case isn't going to look very good. You're not very financially stable to provide for our child."

It wasn't an outright admission, and there was no way to start a recording on her phone. A recording wouldn't be admissible in court either way. This wasn't evidence. But she *knew.*

Banana Bread padded into the kitchen, laying her head on Cayla's knee with a whine. She curled her hand in the dog's fur, appreciating the support. "And what would you know about my financial situation?"

She could practically hear him smile. "Enough. Unfortunately, these sorts of things usually get worse long before they get better. Bad luck seems to spread like a virus."

Was that a threat? It sounded like a threat. Did he mean he could make the situation worse for her? Or was he talking about expanding his targets, going after more people in her circle?

"There is one way to fix it," he continued.

"And what's that?"

"I can make all this go away. I'm good at making things go away. All you have to do is agree to come back to me and bring our daughter with you. I'll wave my magic wand and everybody's happy. You're back where you belong; I get a chance to get to know my daughter; and the cripple and his little friends can go back to their little bakery. It can rise or fall on its own. I don't actually care. They've got enough problems without me needing to add to them. Think about it, sweetheart. I'll be waiting for your answer."

He hung up before she could reply.

For a moment, fury burned through her so bright and hot she couldn't hear a thing. This arrogant, entitled asshole had done everything he could to back her into a corner. And he'd succeeded. She knew exactly how much worse he could make it on her. How much worse he'd made it for other people before she'd sent him away. She was out of options. Because he'd keep doing what he was doing, attacking everyone connected to her, not giving a damn that they weren't actually involved. He didn't care about collateral damage.

But she had to care. She couldn't allow this to continue. Couldn't allow more people to be hurt on her behalf. Not when she was the one person who actually had the power to end this.

But could she actually *do* it? Go back to him? She'd never stay, but maybe she could get close enough, ingratiate herself back into his life far enough to get the information the authorities needed. Except Arthur wasn't a stupid man. He wasn't going to be careless again. And there was the issue of Maddie. If it was just Cayla herself, she might do it in the name of the greater good. But in no universe could she imagine willingly exposing her daughter to that man.

Which left her where?

Holt appeared in the doorway to the kitchen. "I just—What happened?" He hurried across the room. "Cayla? Honey?"

BB lowered to her haunches nearby, her tail giving an uncertain thump as she looked back and forth between them.

Cayla sucked in a slow breath and told him, her voice a flat monotone. Because all the fight had gone out of her.

Holt dropped into a chair and took her hands. "We're going to figure this out. It's going to be okay."

"No, it's not," she whispered. She understood that now.

"What are you talking about?"

She extracted her hands, folding them tight in her lap as she fought back tears. Because she didn't want to say any of this, and she knew what she wanted no longer mattered. "You took on this battle because you believed that you could protect us from whatever he did. But he's not an insurgent. He's not someone posing a physical threat. This isn't a war you can win."

Cayla watched the shutters come down over his eyes and hated herself.

"What are you saying?"

"He holds all the cards. I have no doubt he'll ruin the lives of every single person around me. Where's it going to stop? The FBI doesn't have any more leads or enough information to actually get him off the street and stop him. You've seen how much damage he's done in just six weeks. What if he goes after my mother next? After Jonah's mother? After your sister? After who knows who all of my business contacts? He can and will destroy everything. I can't live with myself if I let him do that."

Holt's blue eyes turned glacial, his hands curling to fists. "You're not going back to him."

"No. No, I'd never expose Maddie to that." And she was shamed enough by the fact that she'd considered it, even for a moment.

"So... what?" he demanded.

"I don't know!" Her shout echoed through the kitchen. She sucked in a breath, swiping at the tears that burned down her cheeks. "I don't know anything except that nothing and no one is safe, and apparently no one can stop him." Holt would realize it, too, sooner or later. And he'd hate her for all the ways she'd ruined his life.

"You can't just give up."

When he reached for her, Cayla rose and stepped back. She couldn't bear him touching her right now. She had to find the strength to stand on her own again, before he cut his losses and walked away.

"I can't live like this. Every day full of dread, waiting for the next bomb to drop." She reached for her purse.

"Where are you going?" There was temper and something that sounded a lot like fear under the question.

"To pick up my child from school and to pray for a fucking miracle. Because I don't see any other way out of this."

Without another word, she strode out, leaving her bruised and battered heart behind.

~

"SHE'S GIVING UP." Holt laced his fingers behind his head and paced another tight circuit of Brax and Mia's living room. He needed to do something. Preferably something that would eliminate the threat Cayla's ex-husband posed. Permanently.

"Okay, you look about two steps away from a berserker rage. Maybe you ought to start at the beginning now that we're all here," Brax said evenly.

With the part of his brain that wasn't currently plotting Raynor's demise, Holt appreciated his friends' rapid response to the SOS he'd sent out. Jonah sat in the armchair, elbows braced on his knees. Brax and Mia occupied the sofa, sitting thigh-to-thigh, as they often did since reconciling. As if, after all those lost years, they couldn't bear to be even that far apart if they were in the same space.

He'd found that with Cayla and damned if he was willing to give it up.

Sucking in a breath, Holt struggled to get a lock on his temper. This wasn't him. He was trained to stay in control. To remain emotionally numb. Objective. But there wasn't a part of him that had been emotionally numb since the moment Maddie had kissed his bad knee above the prosthesis to make the boo boo better. And he hadn't been truly objective since he'd said, "I do." They'd both gotten under his skin and well into his heart.

"The bastard called her this afternoon, after we jumped through all the hoops to report the latest fraud for both her and Maddie. He's basically given her an ultimatum: she comes back to him and brings Maddie, or he continues to expand his reign of terror, indiscriminately financially ruining everyone she touches."

"Wait, did he actually say that?" Jonah demanded.

"He alluded to it, but the message was clear enough. And Cayla believes him."

"She's not actually going to go back to him," Mia insisted. "She'd never do that."

"No. But I've never seen her like this before. It's bad. I don't know what she might do—what the guilt and the desperation might drive her to." He speared both hands into his hair and tugged. "I swore I'd protect them both, and I've failed."

"Man, it's more complicated than that," Brax put in.

"No, it's not. This was the mission I gave myself, and it's gone all kinds of sideways. He came at us in ways I wasn't prepared for. And the consequences for that oversight may be our business and my family."

If they were surprised at the claim, no one voiced it. Because this was no longer a mission. No longer pretend. This was his life. His wife. His child. And he didn't know what to do to save them all.

Mia sat forward. "Have you two spoken to an attorney yet? Does he actually have a case for winning custody?"

"We don't know. We haven't gotten that far yet. We've got a meeting with somebody in Johnson City tomorrow."

"I think I can get you an answer tonight. Let me call Maggie."

Holt frowned. "Porter's wife? I thought she did something with running the small business incubator thing."

"She does. But she's also an Ivy-League-educated attorney. She doesn't have an active legal practice in Tennessee, but she could at least give the opinion of a trained legal professional."

The cool-eyed blonde showed up fifteen minutes later. "How can I help?"

Holt took her through it with considerably more calm and less profanity, explaining the whole situation: how Raynor was out of prison, how that had prompted Holt and Cayla to get married, all Raynor's suspected illegal activities, and how he was suing for full custody. "Does he really have a case?"

"Do you have the paperwork with you?"

"Not on me. I can get it. We just live a little down the street."

"I can't make any definitive claims without reading it, *but* I will say that this is just the initial petition. You and Cayla will respond to the claims, and that opens up a dialogue of sorts— mostly through your attorneys—until both sides mutually agree on terms or a court date is set. Even if your financial situation is problematic, it's been documented that you've been victims of fraud. That isn't necessarily a black mark for you. I mean, of course, it's awful that you're having to go through it, but it's not an automatic mark in his favor. The fact is, in most cases, judges will side with the mother. He'd have to show evidence proving abuse or profound neglect to wrangle full custody. That's simply not going to happen. You're both active, engaged, loving parents, and there are many, many people who'd testify to that fact. Whether he has a case to push for some sort of visitation rights, I can't say. But I think that's the worst you have to fear regarding a custody suit."

A little of the crazed fear leeched out. "Okay. Thank you." Holt let out a slow breath. "So, what are we supposed to do about the rest of it? Cayla's resigned. She feels like nobody is going to be able to stop this fucker. Everybody who was supposed to protect her has failed. Including me. I'm this close to hunting his ass down and finding a deep, dark hole to hide the body."

Maggie covered her ears. "I didn't hear that." She moved toward the door. "I'm getting out of here so I can retain plausible deniability. I've got to go pick up Faith from daycare, anyway."

"Thank you for coming. It gives me a little more peace of mind over all this."

She laid a hand on his arm and offered a sympathetic smile. "Anytime. I hope all this gets straightened out soon."

"You and me both."

Once she was gone, Brax stood. "Raynor doesn't have much of a custody case, so he's using a form of psychological warfare to press other points of leverage. An emotional terrorist trying to break her down on every level."

Holt resumed his pacing. "He's just going to keep at it until the cops catch him, or until somebody beats him at his own game."

Jonah rose to join him. "Okay, so let's think that through. What is his game? What does he want?"

"Control. Power. He's the kind of guy who enjoys playing God. Manipulating everybody around him. He thinks he's the smartest guy in the room. And that's not entirely without merit or he wouldn't have pulled off what he has. But the guy's not infallible. The more people he targets, the more likely he is to make some kind of mistake."

"So, how do we get him to make that mistake?" Brax asked.

Holt stopped pacing, the fragments of a plan beginning to

coalesce in his brain. "We make him think he's getting what he wants."

Mia frowned. "How do we do that?"

"We think like he does." He grabbed his phone. "I need to make some calls."

17

"In my professional opinion, he doesn't have much of a case." Tanika Nowak leaned back in her chair, crossing long legs and clasping her manicured hands in her lap. With her impeccable makeup, cap of short, dark hair, and the ivory pantsuit that highlighted her warm brown skin, she was the picture of confidence, even without the diplomas from UVA and Harvard on her wall. "Even if precedent didn't dictate that mothers overwhelmingly win custody battles, a judge is going to take circumstances into account. You've both been documented victims of identity theft and fraud of the exact same variety that Mr. Raynor went to prison for. Even if that original conviction was appealed, it doesn't take a genius to put two and two together. It's not like the timing was subtle."

"What about that whole innocent until proven guilty thing?" Cayla asked.

Tanika waved her hand. "Those are instructions given to juries in an effort to promote impartiality. Mr. Raynor isn't on trial here. There's no jury involved. And he *was* proven guilty on those counts. I can't imagine any judge awarding him custody. Not without irrefutable evidence that y'all are unfit parents, which I feel certain doesn't exist. A hard-working long-term single mother and a decorated war hero? The only possible angle I can think of that he might try to argue could be some kind of psychological issue on Mr. Steele's part."

Holt sat ramrod straight, unmoving in the chair beside her, as if he were on trial himself or testifying to his Army superiors. "Dr. Audrey Graham, the therapist in charge of my program, will be happy to testify as to the stability of my mental health."

"Then they have nothing."

"What about visitation?" he demanded.

Tanika angled her head, conceding the point. "That's harder. His crimes weren't violent, so it's harder to make a case to keep her from him entirely. But we can certainly fight to limit it to supervised visitation. Since the FBI is still working on gathering evidence for the retrial, my inclination would be to use delay tactics to stretch out the process as long as possible before we go in front of a judge. The bottom line is, you aren't in this alone, and you don't have to worry about losing your daughter."

Cayla relaxed the death grip she had on her hands. Her fingers tingled as blood rushed back into them. "How long are we talking?"

"Easily a few months. And if we need to, I can stretch it out up to a year, most likely. A veritable death by a thousand paper cuts, as it were."

A year. The idea of being embroiled in this mess that much longer made Cayla physically ill. How many more people would Arthur drag down in the meantime because he wasn't getting his way? And he wouldn't be getting his way. Not now. Not ever. But that didn't make living with the consequences any easier.

"There's just one more thing." Cayla renewed the strangled tangle of her fingers. "If we do this and it stretches on that long, there's the matter of billing. How would that be handled? Given the current restraints of our situation because of the fraud investigation, that's something of an issue."

Tanika's velvety brown eyes softened. "We'll do it however you need to. Hell, we'll ask for attorney's fees because he's brought a nuisance suit to waste everyone's time."

"Will that work?" Holt asked.

"I mean, stranger things have happened. But even if they say no, we'll make whatever arrangements are necessary, whatever kind of payment plan you need, until they sort things out for you."

Cayla struggled to keep her shoulders straight and maintain eye contact. "And if it's years?"

"Then it's years." Tanika shrugged. "I'll still win this battle for you. Trust me, honey, I've taken payment in the form of fresh eggs and turnip greens before. I'm not worried."

Humbled by the other woman's kindness and buoyed by her confidence, Cayla nodded. "Thank you. Then we'd appreciate it if you would take the case."

They stayed a while longer, going over the particulars of what information Tanika needed to formulate their initial reply to the petition. When they left her office, it was nearing the end of the school day. As they hadn't known how long they'd be in Johnson City, Donna was picking Maddie up and taking her back to the house. Cayla was grateful for the near hour's drive to pull herself together. She felt brittle and bruised, and she was so very aware of the need to present a picture of normalcy for her child, even though it felt as if her world was falling apart.

She didn't know how to do that with the man sitting next to her in the driver's seat. Holt kept his eyes fixed on the road, his jaw set. He'd been entirely shut down, back to the distant, taciturn soldier she'd seen when he first arrived. But he'd never been that way with her before.

She'd hurt him yesterday. For all the things unspoken

between them, she knew that beyond the shadow of a doubt. In her despair, she'd essentially thrown everything he'd done for her and Maddie back in his face as worthless. It wasn't worthless. Despite the inherent stress of their circumstances, the past several weeks with him had been so much more than she could've hoped. She'd truly believed that they were building something real and lasting.

Now it felt as if the man she'd come to love was a stranger.

She'd been the one to do the hurting, so she was the one who had to make amends. Not knowing how to broach the topic, she glanced in his direction. "I'm sorry about last night."

A muscle jumped in his jaw, but he said nothing.

Cayla gripped her fingers again. "I overreacted in the moment. I was upset and felt cornered. And I... I'm just so sick to death of empty assurances everything's going to be okay. Because right now, I don't see how. It feels like nothing can be done to stop him, and that terrifies me. Knowing the full scope of what he can bring down on the people I love, what he *has* brought down—I don't know how to live with the burden of knowing I'm the reason he's targeted everyone."

The tightening of his hands on the wheel was the only sign he was listening.

"But I'm going to have to learn how to live with it. Because there's no reality where I'd sacrifice Maddie. Not even if he burns the world."

Holt's exhale was slow and controlled, a clear releasing of tension. "Good."

That single word was his only response. He didn't even look at her.

God, did he really believe she was capable of doing that? Had he truly been worried she'd go that far?

Heart breaking, Cayla suffered his silence the rest of the drive back to Eden's Ridge, wondering if she'd destroyed her marriage with her lack of faith. Then again, was it a real marriage at all if it could be so easily broken? She'd come up with no answers by the time he pulled into the driveway at the house.

He parked outside the garage and finally deigned to look at her. "I'm gonna drop you off. I need to catch up on some work at the bakery."

There was nothing of the warmth she'd come to expect in his vivid blue eyes. No hint of forgiveness. But maybe he needed more time to process on his own.

"All right. Do you think you'll be home for dinner?"

"I'll probably be working late."

Eyes burning, Cayla just nodded and slipped out of the SUV.

Without another word, he drove away.

IN THE BAKERY KITCHEN, Holt kneaded fondant, working in the blue food coloring with hard, almost violent strokes. He'd have felt better with a gun or knife in his hands, but this fight with Arthur Raynor wasn't the kind he'd been trained for. To end this, he had to play a different sort of game. One that went against most of his better instincts. But the plan was solid, all the pieces in place, with multiple fail-safes. He refused to believe that Raynor was smarter than the team he'd put together to do this.

He just had to get through tonight. Then he could go home and make up with his wife. The drive back from Johnson City had been awful. Everything in him had wanted to comfort Cayla. To pull the 4-Runner over, drag her into his arms, and erase the distance between them. But just in case Raynor was watching them, it needed to look like they were rocky. Everything hinged on that.

Holt checked the clock. Nearing nine. Almost showtime.

The air in the kitchen was stuffy, so he propped open the back door to let in some of the cool night breeze. Music played over the Bluetooth speaker. No show tunes or Disney tonight. The driving rock kept his blood up, ready for action, though it was highly unlikely Raynor would give him a reasonable opportunity to use his fists. More was the pity. He'd relish the chance to take the guy on in an honest, man-to-man brawl. A guy like that wouldn't last a minute. He had soft hands. The kind that probably didn't even know how to make a real fist. No, Raynor preferred to take on unsuspecting victims. Innocents. All so he could maintain his attitude of total superiority. Holt had to remember that and cater to it.

If the asshole actually showed.

God, he hoped he was doing the right thing.

The front door opened right at nine. The guy was prompt.

Holt continued working the fondant as Raynor glanced around the front, taking it in as if he'd never seen it before. His expression said he wasn't impressed. That wasn't Holt's concern.

"Come on back." He jerked his head toward the swinging door.

Arthur pushed through. He wore dress pants and a button-down shirt that fit him so impeccably that they had to be tailored. His brown dress shoes were polished to a gleam and squeaked with every step. He stopped just inside the kitchen, his gold eyes scanning the room with clear contempt.

"Thank you for coming."

"I have to admit, I was surprised to hear from you."

I'll bet you were.

As the fondant was now a consistent robin's egg blue, Holt folded it in plastic wrap and stripped off his gloves before putting it in the cooler. He let the door fall shut with a thump. "Yeah, well, you haven't left me a lot of choice. So I figured we'd handle this man-to-man."

A glint of intrigue lit Raynor's otherwise bland expression. "I'm listening." He pulled something out of his pocket. A coin of some kind. He began to walk it from knuckle to knuckle on his left hand.

Needing to keep moving, Holt wiped down his workstation. "I'm ceding the field."

One blond brow arched up. "I beg your pardon?"

"I'm pulling out of this whole situation. I've seen what you can do. You've cut me and my business partners off at the damned knees."

The other man's lips twitched. "It appears someone else got there first."

Holt didn't allow himself to react to the jab. A guy like this would absolutely see him as less, as broken. Now wasn't the time to prove him wrong. He had to play exactly as Raynor saw him. So thinking, he limped a little as he moved around the table, wiping away debris.

"Cayla was yours first. The kid's yours. They're not worth losing my future, my business. And I can't afford for you to decide to go after my sister. God knows Hadley's just gotten on her feet. I'm not gonna be the reason she fails. And I can't risk you going after my surrogate mother or anybody else I care about. They were in my life first. They'll be in my life last. I'm not losing everything over a woman or a brat that's not mine. So I'm letting you know I'm out. You've won."

Raynor's lips curved, the unholy light of victory brightening his face. "And why did you bring me out here for that?"

"Because I knew you'd want to look into my face as I had to admit I wish I'd never gotten involved with them in the first place." And Holt let the frustration and irritation at that show. For all the man thought him less, he'd understand that such an admission would be a blow to Holt's pride. "And because I want to make a deal."

"A deal?" Faint surprise crept into that upper crust voice.

"You don't seem to be in a position to negotiate. What do you have that I want?"

Throughout the conversation, Holt had hoped Raynor would say something that qualified as an admission of guilt. But as he'd expected, the guy was too careful for that. So he braced himself to pull the metaphorical trigger and do the thing he'd come here to do. "I'm in your way. As long as Cayla thinks she has me, she'll hold out against you. But if that's taken away? She folds. She's already so damned close."

Arthur hummed a noncommittal note. "So you're suggesting that you will get out of my way in exchange for...?"

"Money. Ten grand. It's not a lot in the grand scheme of things. Certainly to a guy like you. But it's enough to save my business. Transfer it to me tonight, and I'll make it easy on you and file for divorce tomorrow."

The hissed breath came from behind him, and Holt knew even before he heard her voice.

"How could you?"

Fuck.

He turned, catching one glimpse of Cayla's ashen, horrified face in the open doorway before she backed away and ran. Her steps echoed on the wood planks of the wrap-around porch.

Everything in him wanted to race after her. But if he did, all this would probably be for nothing. He had to stick to the plan.

With a sigh, he turned back to face Raynor, who appeared infinitely amused by the proceedings.

"That changes nothing," Holt began.

The other man laughed. "Oh, you are delusional. I don't need you to do anything. She'll do it on her own. But I do thank you for the show." He turned to go.

"Wait!"

With a bored air, he looked back. "What?"

"Forget the money. Can I at least have your assurance you won't touch anybody else connected to me? You got what you want. Me out of the way. There's no reason for you to target them."

Raynor merely huffed another laugh and walked out.

Holt forced himself to wait until the front door had closed. He shut off the speaker and listened for the sound of a car engine driving away. The moment Raynor was gone, he was dialing Cayla's number.

Of course, she didn't answer.

He let out a stream of curses until the voicemail kicked on. "Cayla, honey, it's not what you think. I swear, it's not. Just give me a chance to explain."

The moment he hung up, he sent her a text to the same effect.

But no reply was forthcoming. Hell, she was probably still driving. But to where? Not home. He could only assume that Donna, or possibly Mia, was at the house with Maddie. She wouldn't take this upset to where her daughter would see.

Think, think, think.

Where the hell would she go? Panic bubbled just beneath the surface as he reviewed the options and came up with nothing.

Locking the doors, he quickly set the alarm and dove into his 4-Runner, intent on tracking down his wife before she did something neither of them could take back.

18

C ayla was sobbing so hard, it was a miracle she made it up the mountain. When she saw the outside lights weren't on, she almost collapsed into a puddle of defeated misery. But it looked like there were lights inside, so she stumbled out of her car and to the front door. Misty had to be home. If she wasn't... well, Cayla hadn't thought that far ahead.

The light on the front porch came on and the door swung open. Denver Hershel, Misty's fiancé, took one look at the tears streaming down Cayla's face and lost at least two shades of color from his own. With clear I-don't-know-what-to-do-with-female-tears panic in his eyes, he shouted, "Misty!"

A few moments later, Misty's head appeared past Denver's shoulder. "Oh dear God." She hurried outside, wrapping her arms around Cayla in a tight hug.

At the kind touch, Cayla lost hold of whatever scraps of control she'd had and the sobbing cranked up again, uncontrollable. Misty just held on, not offering reassurances or platitudes. Eventually, she steered Cayla into the house, nudging her toward the living room and down onto the sofa without letting go.

"Do you want some tea? Something stronger?"

Because she couldn't speak, Cayla just shook her head. When a bottle of water appeared in her line of vision a minute later, she glanced up at a grim-faced Denver. Taking the bottle, she sniffled, "Thanks."

With shaking hands, she opened the water and drank, the cold liquid soothing her burning throat.

"What happened? Is it Arthur?"

"Yes. No. I... don't know." Her thoughts were too scattered, her mind shying away from the truth of what she'd heard. She drank more water and tried to pull herself together enough to explain herself.

"Arthur is suing for full custody of Maddie."

"Oh, shit. That's what you were afraid of, right?"

"As it turns out, that's the least of it. Things have gotten... bad." She laid it out as best she could. "On the way home, I tried to apologize and talk to Holt about the fight, but he wouldn't even look at me. He dropped me off at the house and said he'd be working late. I stewed about it for a while and eventually called my mom to come stay with Maddie so I could go up and talk to him. I wanted to clear the air because I can't stand where we are right now."

Her throat threatened to close up again as fresh tears welled. "And when I got there, Arthur was there, and Holt was making a deal with him to divorce me for money."

Misty's jaw dropped. "I'm sorry, what?"

"You heard me."

"That can't possibly be right. I know your marriage started under unconventional circumstances, but I just can't fathom him doing something like that."

"Neither could I." Not in her wildest nightmares. "But I heard it with my own two ears. I walked in on this conversation, and Holt turned around and looked at me, and he didn't say a word." Not one word. Not one blink or change in expression to indicate regret or guilt or secret assurances that it wasn't really what it looked like.

"Okay, that's bad," Misty conceded. "But it doesn't make any sense. Why would Holt do that?"

It didn't make sense. It didn't at all match up with the man she thought she knew. But she didn't know how else to explain what she'd seen and heard. "I mean, Arthur's done everything he can to ruin us. To ruin all three of them. He wants to save his business, I guess. I wondered what it was going to take for him to regret marrying me. Where his line would be. I guess now I know." And she'd probably been the one to push him over it when she'd lost faith in him. In them.

Misty took her hand and squeezed in sympathy.

Someone pounded on the front door.

"Holt." It had to be. Who else would be knocking hard enough to sound like the big bad wolf?

Denver rose to his full height, crossing big, tattooed arms. "Do you want me to get rid of him?"

He was a sizable guy. Nearly Holt's height and close to his weight. But Holt had considerably more training and Cayla had no idea what his mental state was. Before she could answer, Misty spoke up. "He tracked you down for a reason. Maybe give him a chance to offer some kind of explanation? Then, if you want us to throw him out, we can throw him out."

Desperate for any scrap of possibility that this was all some horrific mistake, Cayla nodded. "Okay."

Denver answered the door.

"Where is she?" There wasn't a trace of calm in Holt's tone.

"I don't know what's going on, but you'll hold your shit together or you won't be coming into my house," Denver informed him.

"Fine. Let me see her. Please." This last was gritted out.

Denver stepped back. As soon as he was through the door, Holt made a beeline for the living room. This wasn't the cold, distant soldier she'd seen for the past couple of days. Wasn't the expressionless pod person who'd stood in the bakery kitchen and looked through her. Outright panic was written across his features. It was so unexpected, so unlike him, Cayla almost asked *him* what was wrong.

At the sight of her, he loosed a ragged breath, visibly relaxing. "Thank God, you're okay."

The absurdity of the statement cut through the devastation and had her sputtering in disbelief. "Okay? Really?"

He held up his hands, palms out. "Not what I meant. I just —Look, I know what you walked in on looked bad. But it wasn't what you think."

It was exactly what she'd wanted him to say. Combined with the uncharacteristic show of vulnerability, a fragile ember of hope began to glow. She'd been wrong before. She'd misjudged situations with him before. Maybe, somehow, some way, there was a viable reason for his actions. Cayla wanted to believe there was because she wasn't ready for their marriage to be over.

Misty rose. "We're just gonna give you two some privacy." Grabbing Denver by the arm, she towed him from the room.

Not wanting to face whatever was coming sitting down, Cayla shoved up from the sofa. "And what is it you think I think?"

"That I betrayed you. That I meant anything I said to him." Holt took a step closer. "I didn't. The whole thing was a sting operation."

Whatever she'd expected him to say, it hadn't been that. "It was what?"

"A sting operation. The only way to make Arthur stop is to make him think he's getting what he wants. He's an arrogant son of a bitch. If he thinks he's won, he's more likely to get careless enough to make a mistake. So I decided to play to that arrogance. I talked to Hadley and Rebecca. We set them up as deliberate targets, trying to get him to go after their accounts, their information, to do the same thing to them. I had to meet with him to plant both of them as potential targets. To make it seem like I was desperate to keep him from going after them. Because that's exactly what we want him to do."

The idea of deliberately baiting Arthur to go after people they cared about had her chest seizing. "Why would you want him to do that? And who is 'we'?"

"Remember, I told you my buddy Cash used to be Army Intelligence?"

"Yeah. You said he's in cybersecurity now."

"He is. He's also a consultant for the FBI, among other alphabet soup agencies. I put him in touch with Special Agent Marquez. He's got a mechanism in place—don't ask me what, I don't understand all the ins and outs of that hacker shit—so when Arthur goes after either them, we get access to his system, and the FBI can get everything they need to prove that he's been behind all of this shit from the beginning. So he can get sent back to prison. You just happened to show up in the middle of the whole damned thing, and I couldn't break character to come after you until he was gone."

He'd edged closer through the whole explanation until he was standing close enough she could feel the heat of him.

"You said you couldn't live like this anymore. Neither could I. This is probably more of a Hail Mary than a miracle, but it's what we've got. And I'm so sorry that you heard that. I'm so damned sorry that, for even a single moment, you thought that was the truth. I love you, and I'd never, ever deliberately hurt you like that."

Cayla stared up at him, her mind spinning through everything he'd just said. He'd given her the impossible. A rational explanation. One that meant their marriage wasn't a lie. And he'd given her something even bigger than that.

"You love me?" It was everything she'd hoped for but hadn't let herself truly believe was possible.

His brows drew together. "Have I done that shitty a job of showing you?"

She barked out something halfway between a cry and a laugh. "No. No, you haven't." Because everything he'd done, every action he'd taken, had been a silent declaration she hadn't been ready to trust. But after all this, how could she ever do anything else?

Holt framed her face between his broad palms. "Then let me be perfectly clear. I love you. I am in love with you. I am in love with our daughter. And I don't want to let either of you go. Ever."

Relief and joy were a tangle inside the heart that was suddenly beating again. She flowed into him, wrapping her arms around his waist. "I love you, too."

"Thank Christ."

Holt's mouth found hers, and his kiss tasted of relief and desperation. Cayla held on, pressing closer, even as his arms banded tight enough to squeeze her breath. She didn't care, so long as he never, ever let her go again.

"I thought I'd lost you," he murmured.

"I thought you didn't want me anymore. That I'd driven you away with my lack of faith. Of trust. I'm so sorry I hurt you."

Holt combed the hair back from her face. "You have nothing to apologize for. We've both got issues and sore spots. Those are challenging enough in a normal relationship under the best of circumstances. These past weeks haven't been the best of circumstances. The important thing is that he didn't break us. No matter what else he pulls, no matter how powerful he seems to be, he can't do that. We won't let him."

Cayla tightened her hold as she looked up into those beloved blue eyes. "No. We won't let him do that."

Someone cleared their throat. "I mean, this is touching and all, but am I the only one who wants to know if it worked?"

"Denver!" Misty hissed.

"Sorry, but they're not exactly quiet, and I'm invested now."

Cayla dropped her head to Holt's chest with a watery laugh before pulling back just far enough to look up at him. "*Did* it work? Or did I screw everything up? Was it all for nothing?"

"Honestly, I don't know. We'll just have to see what happens. Unfortunately, it's probably going to be another waiting game."

She was so very tired of waiting.

The phone in his back pocket began to ring.

Keeping one arm around her, Holt fished it out. "It's Cash."

"Put it on speaker," Cayla urged.

"Hey. You're on speaker. Tell me you've got something."

"Bet your ass I do." Cayla had no idea what Cash looked like, but even she could hear the smug grin in his voice. "The bastard didn't wait twenty minutes before going after Hadley. I've got a back door into his entire system and access to everything he has. He's officially locked down. Can't hurt anybody else. I'll be transferring all the information to the FBI in short order."

"Really? Does that mean it's over?" She hardly dared to believe it.

"This son of a bitch is going back to prison real soon."

"And he wasn't able to actually touch Hadley's information?" Holt confirmed.

"What do you take me for? I promised she'd be safe. She's safe."

A woman's voice came over the line. "Don't insult the man, Holt."

He tensed. "Why is my sister there with you?"

"Like I was going to sit out on a sting? This is the most exciting thing that's happened to me in ages. Our boy, Cash, is a computer genius."

"Why, thank you, madam."

"Don't let it go to your head," Hadley told him. "I have way too many stories about you from when we were kids to see you as anything other than a mere mortal."

"I've got plenty more on you."

"Mutually assured destruction," Hadley said cheerfully. "We're gonna go now and let you finish making up with your wife. Bye, Cayla!"

There was something in their banter that had Cayla wondering if there was more between them than a lifelong friendship. But given Holt's reaction, she kept the question to herself.

When the line went dead, Holt stared at the phone for a moment before shoving it back in his pocket. "Well, that was... faster than I expected. Also, a little anticlimactic."

"Wishing you were there for the takedown?"

"For the chance to plant my fist in his face for all the pain and suffering he's caused us and everyone else? Hell yeah. But that wasn't my role to play in this."

"You stepped way out of your comfort zone to put an end to this whole nightmare. And it worked. I don't know how to thank you for that."

"I protect what's mine. You and Maddie are mine." His smile turned a little wicked. "But if you're feeling like you have to express gratitude, I've got some ideas."

Cayla linked her arms around his neck. "Then let's go home, warrior mine."

"Can I go outside to play with Banana Bread some more?" Maddie folded her hands in a prayer position. "Pleeeeeease, Daddy?"

As if Holt could refuse her anything when she called him Daddy? "Well, since school is *officially* out for the summer and you don't have to be up and out first thing tomorrow, I suppose you can have a little more playtime."

"Thank you!" Without giving him a chance to change his mind, she bolted out the backdoor, BB on her heels, into the newly fenced backyard.

Cayla huffed a laugh.

"What?" he asked.

"She's totally figured you out. Hit you with those big brown eyes and call you Daddy, and you'll agree to almost anything."

"I fit quite neatly around her little finger. I admit it." Holt snagged his wife around the waist and nuzzled her neck. "I'm just as big a softie for her mama."

Cayla's hand skated down his back to cop a friendly squeeze of his ass. "Well, maybe softie isn't the right word."

Even as he hummed a note of approval, the doorbell was ringing.

She frowned. "It's nearly eight. Who's stopping by this late?"

Holt strode to the front door and pulled it open. The man on the front stoop was a Fed. Holt recognized that from the suit and the stance before he even took in the guy's salt and pepper hair and the bronze skin that hinted at some kind of Hispanic ancestry.

"Mr. Steele. I'm Special Agent Anthony Marquez. May I come in?"

Holt's first instinct was to bar the door to whatever bad news this guy might carry. But his manner was easy, with no suggestion of dread in his posture.

"Sure."

Cayla stepped into the room. "Special Agent Marquez!"

"Ms. Black." He stepped into the house, frowning. "Or is it Mrs. Steele now?"

Oh, Holt liked the sound of that.

"How about Cayla? I feel like maybe we're past the formalities at this point."

"Fair enough. Please call me Anthony. I'm sorry to stop by so late, but I had some news."

Holt automatically reached for her, stepping close to be brace or shield as necessary, though he didn't really think it was bad. "Why don't we step out back? Maddie's out there playing. We want to keep an eye on her."

"Of course." Marquez followed them out to the back porch.

Maddie was out in the yard, playing some bastardized version of fetch with the dog where she threw a ball and they both chased after it. Her delighted giggles filled the air. For a moment, they all watched her and smiled. It was hard not to. She was the picture of childhood innocence. They'd managed to preserve that for her.

At last, the agent turned to face them. "I'll get straight to the point. Arthur Raynor is officially back in prison, and we've got all the evidence we need to keep him there this time. He will still face trial for the additional counts of fraud that he committed while he was out. I wanted to personally let you both know that I'm pulling some strings to fast track getting the fraud cleared from your records and those of your friends. It will still take a little time, but everything should be sorted by the end of the month. I apologize for how long it took, and for the fact that he was out to cause trouble in the first place."

Cayla sucked in a breath. "So, it's really over?"

"It's really, really over," Marquez confirmed.

"Thank you." She shook the agent's hand and held it for a moment. "Truly. I know I was a little hard on you at the end there."

Marquez waved that off. "Completely understandable. I

didn't take it personally. And anyway, you weren't wrong. We wouldn't have tied things up quite so neatly without your husband's help, and that of his... associate."

That was a polite way of saying he wasn't sure who the hell Cash was, but he wasn't looking the gift of good intel in the mouth.

"He's a handy guy to know."

The older man's lips twitched. "Let's just say we're glad he's on our side. Anyway, I just wanted to come by and let you know in person. You've certainly earned that. I'll let you folks get back to your evening."

After he was gone, they settled on the swing, thigh to thigh, as the last rays of sun faded from the watercolor sky. Maddie continued to romp with Banana Bread, now switching to chasing the fireflies winking on and off. He put his arm around Cayla, and she snuggled close against him. For long minutes, they sat in silence, and Holt absorbed everything about this little slice of contentment.

"Has it sunk in yet?"

She glanced up. "I don't know if it's ever really going to sink in. I think there's always going to be a piece of me that worries Arthur might get out again and try to pull the same stunts."

"Oh, even if he does, he won't be able to pull off what he pulled off again. Cash has set up the mac daddy of all identity protection services on all of us. But I don't think he's gonna get out for a very long time."

Her sigh was full of relief, but her silence was full of something else.

"What's on your mind?"

"I don't know. I guess I'm thinking about what's next."

Holt definitely had some ideas about that. "What did you have in mind?"

Tearing her gaze away from Maddie, she looked up at him, face serious. "Are you really happy being a family man? I mean, you jumped into this for honorable reasons. And those reasons are now resolved."

"Are you seriously trying to give me an out?"

"I mean, it's only fair. We haven't ever had the chance to think about us without Arthur in the equation. So I'm thinking about it now."

He didn't get any kind of sense that she wasn't happy with them being an "us", so he took a moment to consider how best to reassure her.

"Marrying you and becoming a family man was the best decision I've ever made. I was kind of thinking I'd like to do it all over again."

She blinked in surprise. "You want to get married again?"

He stopped toying with the ends of her hair to trace a finger across the bare patch of skin exposed by her tank top. "No, I'm fine with what we did as long as you are. Though if you wanted to change your name, that'd be cool."

"I would love to be officially Mrs. Holt Steele." Her sexy smile gave him the confidence to push on with the rest of it.

"And I want to adopt Maddie. Officially. I don't want her to ever have reason to think she's not wanted. And on the unlikely chance Arthur ever comes back, I want to have the rights to do something about it."

Her dark eyes gleamed with happy tears. "Yes, absolutely. She's already yours."

"And..."

"There's more?" she teased.

He traced that finger lower on her shoulder. "Then I was thinking more along the lines of doing the whole family thing again."

For one beat, two, she just stared at him. Then her eyes went dark with realization. "You want to have a baby?"

"Yeah. I want one with you. I want to have all the fun of the trying, and I want to get to be there from the beginning. For the whole thing. What do you say? Do you want to give Maddie a little brother or sister?"

The silence stretched out for so long he wondered if he'd pushed for too much too soon.

"I mean, not like we need to tackle that right away. I know we've had a lot of changes, and we're still getting used to a lot of stuff. But I just thought you should know that's where my brain is headed. If that's something you want."

She leaned in close, dropping her voice low. "Then we both better get much, much better at being really, really quiet."

Holt grinned. "Challenge accepted." And he kissed his wife in the summer twilight with their daughter's laughter in the air.

EPILOGUE

In the veritable sea of blissfully happy couples, Jonah Ferguson stood alone, ever the observer. In all their wedding finery, Brax and Mia led the crowd in the "Cha Cha Slide" on the dance floor set up out in the new yard at the house they still weren't quite done renovating. Even a jaded bastard like him hadn't been unaffected by watching his friends make their vows all over again. They'd come through so damned much to find their way back to each other, and even though it hadn't been deliberate on his part, Jonah was still pleased about his own role in putting Brax back in Mia's path. His friend was whole again. It was the only way Jonah could think to describe the change he'd seen in Brax.

Holt had succumbed in his own way, taking to married and family life like a duck to water. He had Maddie on one side, Cayla on the other, all of them laughing as they stomped and shook to the music. They made a sweet picture. Not that he'd ever admitted it, but Holt had been thirsty for family, for connection. The brotherhood of the military and the one they'd forged since they all got out only fed a part of him. Cayla and her daughter filled the void in a way no one else could've.

Hell, even Jonah's sister Sam was shaking her very pregnant belly at the edge of the dance floor. Her husband Griff danced beside her with a vaguely terrified expression, as if he was certain all this exercise was going to send her into labor at any moment. Jonah thought it was a valid concern. His baby sister seemed big as a house. Not that he'd tell her that on pain of death. She'd been so deliriously happy since she eloped with Griff—and who the hell had seen that coming? Or the fact that they'd secretly eloped in Vegas before when they'd been twenty-two. Jonah still hadn't quite squared that in his mind, but since Griff seemed to practically worship the ground Sam walked on, he couldn't find a reason to complain.

The people he loved were happy. And Jonah was willing to do a hell of a lot to protect that happiness. He was more and more certain that there was something to protect them from. Ever since Holt had brought up the idea that all the problems they'd faced had been targeting them rather than Mia, Jonah had been chewing on it. He'd reviewed the security footage of the latest vandalism and Holt's meeting with Arthur Raynor. They weren't the same guy. They carried themselves differently. And whoever had been the vandal was right-handed. Raynor was a leftie, something Jonah had confirmed with Cayla. The more he thought about, the more he suspected Holt was partly right. Except it didn't make sense that anyone would target the three of them. Brax and Holt were new here. The trouble started before they'd been around long enough to make any enemies.

No. Now that alternative explanations had been ruled out, Jonah was pretty damned sure it all had something to do with his father. He'd had nothing to do with Lonnie Barker from the time Rebecca had divorced his ass when Jonah was eight, so it had been a big surprise when he'd left the bar to the kids he'd basically abandoned. While The Right Attitude had been popular among a certain hard-drinking set, it certainly wasn't any kind of mass money maker. Over the years, Jonah and his mom had theorized that Lonnie had to be into something else to make money. Jonah hadn't given the specifics of that much thought for a long time. But he was thinking about it now. The man who'd nearly killed Mia had been ranting something about a flash drive. Everything he'd done had been in search of information. If his dad had somehow been involved in something less than above-board, it was entirely possible that whoever his targets or associates had been were worried that the new owners were going to somehow stumble upon the information. Information on what, Jonah had no idea. Blackmail? Money laundering? Drug running? Either way, it made more sense that this had something to do with Lonnie and the less-than-reputable crowd he'd run with most of his life.

"Ten bucks says they've got a bun in the oven by the end of the year."

Startled out of his thoughts, Jonah turned his attention to the tall, gorgeous blonde beside him. "Huh?"

With a half-empty glass of champagne, Rachel gestured toward the dance floor where Holt and Cayla were slow dancing to whatever Ed Sheeran song was playing, completely oblivious to anyone else around them. "Look at them. If looks could cause pregnancy, she'd already have twins."

Jonah eyed her. "How much champagne have you had?"

"Mmm." She sipped more. "Not enough."

It occurred to him that as a widow, this whole vow renewal thing would probably be bringing up a lot of memories. "I guess weddings are kind of hard on you, huh?"

She shrugged slim shoulders. "Yes, and no. I love love. I'm ecstatic to see them happy. And of course, I remember being that happy. It's bittersweet. But every day is a little easier." Making an obvious effort to throw off her mood, she sipped more champagne. "So why are you over here propping up the wall?"

"Somebody's gotta do it."

Her gaze slid up to him with a teasing smile that had his pants going tight. A tall woman to start, in the heels she wore, she didn't have far to go. "Why aren't you out there cutting a rug with a date?"

Jonah shifted subtly to ease the pressure. "I've been too busy with shit since we got down here to worry about finding a woman."

With a pointed glance at their friends, she just arched her brows. "Is it that you don't want a woman in general or that there's just not one you're interested in?"

The woman he wanted was standing right here. But Jonah wasn't going there. He hadn't touched her for the year he'd been in Syracuse because she was a widow and still grieving. As she'd healed, he still hadn't touched her because the life he was building wasn't in New York. She was a forever girl, one who deserved more than long-distance. They'd become close friends. A friend was what she'd needed all this time, and he'd been absolutely determined to be that for her.

Since he wasn't about to give her an honest answer to that question, he turned the tables. "What about you? You didn't bring a date either."

With a grimace, she sipped more champagne. "Dating as a widow is hard. Dating in Syracuse is even harder. There are memories everywhere. So I haven't done it."

"Do you want to date?" Jonah told himself the answer didn't matter.

"I don't even know. John and I were high school sweethearts. I've never dated as an adult. And the whole idea of navigating that is... exhausting. I signed up for online dating and got so many dick picks in twenty-four hours, I deleted my account."

"Stay far, far away from the bottom feeders."

"Believe me, I intend to." Rachel spun the stem of her glass between two fingers. "That said, I know John wouldn't have wanted me to be alone and grieving him the rest of my life. I'm working my way around to doing something about it." She took a bigger gulp of the champagne and sucked in a deep breath. "I was hoping you could help me with that."

Please, God, no. But Jonah kept his face neutral. "You need me to screen some guys? Make sure they're worth your time? That they'll treat you right?"

"No, I've already done that. He is, and he does."

She turned to him, blue eyes searching his face, her own full of something that looked an awful lot like hope and expectation. Except it couldn't possibly be that.

"Then how can I help?"

Her shoulders straightened. She tipped back the last of the champagne and set the glass aside with a thump. "Maybe this will help clarify." And she curved those strong, slender fingers that had taught him everything he knew about baking around his nape, closing the distance between them to lay her lips over his.

Stunned to the marrow, Jonah didn't move as she settled her mouth more firmly against his in a soft, questioning kiss. Rachel McCleary, the object of his every fantasy for the past two years, was kissing him. His brain spun, trying to analyze all the possible actions and outcomes and what the right move would be. But its computing power was hampered by all the blood in his head draining south.

And then she pulled back, far enough he could see the color burning high in her cheeks, distress etched in those blue-bonnet eyes.

Jonah opened his mouth to say—he had no clue what— when his sister's voice cut through the sudden silence between songs.

"Oh, my God! My water just broke!"

I HOPE this grumpy soft for sunshine tale gave you as many warm fuzzies as it did me. I'll be super interested to hear readers debate whether Holt or Caleb from *Let It Be Me* is their favorite unicorn hero. Meanwhile, we've finally reached the final leg of our trilogy with Jonah and Rachels story, *Stirred Up by a SEAL.*

Can a SEAL without a mission and a widowed baker help each other learn to live again?

Jonah Ferguson never wanted to be anything but a Navy SEAL. But after an injury sidelines his military career, he finds himself back home in small-town Tennessee. Opening a bakery with his best friends and daring to re-imagine his life is a whole new mission, but his biggest challenge yet is sticking to the friend zone with the woman who helped give him new purpose.

Two years after losing her husband to a traumatic brain injury, baker Rachel McCleary needs a change. With the proceeds from the sale of her business, she's exploring what a new life would look like. For the short-term, it means helping one of her former students make his fledgling business thrive. And hopefully adding some benefits to the friendship that helped bring her back to life.

All Rachel wants is temporary, and that's the one thing Jonah can give her. But when the trouble that's stalked his business from the start lands her in its crosshairs--and the hospital--he can't deny that there's nothing short-term about his feelings.

Determined to protect her at all costs, he enters into a dangerous race to neutralize the threat before it torpedoes everything he holds dear.

STIRRED Up by a SEAL releases August 5th, and you can preorder your copy today!

OTHER BOOKS BY KAIT NOLAN

A complete and up-to-date list of all my books can be found at https://kaitnolan.com.

∿

THE MISFIT INN SERIES
SMALL TOWN FAMILY ROMANCE

- *When You Got A Good Thing* (Kennedy and Xander)
- *Til There Was You* (Misty and Denver)
- *Those Sweet Words* (Pru and Flynn)
- *Stay A Little Longer* (Athena and Logan)
- *Bring It On Home* (Maggie and Porter)

RESCUE MY HEART SERIES
SMALL TOWN MILITARY ROMANCE

- *Baby It's Cold Outside* (Ivy and Harrison)
- *What I Like About You* (Laurel and Sebastian)
- *Bad Case of Loving You* (Paisley and Ty prequel)

- *Made For Loving You* (Paisley and Ty)

MEN OF THE MISFIT INN
SMALL TOWN SOUTHERN ROMANCE

- *Let It Be Me* (Emerson and Caleb)
- *Our Kind of Love* (Abbey and Kyle)
- *Don't You Wanna Stay* (Deanna and Wyatt)
- *Until We Meet Again* (Samantha and Griffin prequel)
- *Come A Little Closer* (Samantha and Griffin)

BAD BOY BAKERS
SMALL TOWN MILITARY ROMANCE

- *Rescued By a Bad Boy* (Brax and Mia prequel)
- *Mixed Up With a Marine* (Brax and Mia)
- *Wrapped Up with a Ranger* (Holt and Cayla): Coming June 3, 2022)
- *Stirred Up by a SEAL* (Jonah and Rachel): Coming August 5th

WISHFUL ROMANCE SERIES
SMALL TOWN SOUTHERN ROMANCE

- *Once Upon A Coffee* (Avery and Dillon)
- *To Get Me To You* (Cam and Norah)
- *Know Me Well* (Liam and Riley)
- *Be Careful, It's My Heart* (Brody and Tyler)
- *Just For This Moment* (Myles and Piper)
- *Wish I Might* (Reed and Cecily)
- *Turn My World Around* (Tucker and Corinne)
- *Dance Me A Dream* (Jace and Tara)
- *See You Again* (Trey and Sandy)
- *The Christmas Fountain* (Chad and Mary Alice)

- *You Were Meant For Me* (Mitch and Tess)
- *A Lot Like Christmas* (Ryan and Hannah)
- *Dancing Away With My Heart* (Zach and Lexi)

WISHING FOR A HERO SERIES (A WISHFUL SPINOFF SERIES)
SMALL TOWN ROMANTIC SUSPENSE

- *Make You Feel My Love* (Judd and Autumn)
- *Watch Over Me* (Nash and Rowan)
- *Can't Take My Eyes Off You* (Ethan and Miranda)
- *Burn For You* (Sean and Delaney)

MEET CUTE ROMANCE
SMALL TOWN SHORT ROMANCE

- *Once Upon A Snow Day*
- *Once Upon A New Year's Eve*
- *Once Upon An Heirloom*
- *Once Upon A Coffee*
- *Once Upon A Campfire*
- *Once Upon A Rescue*

SUMMER CAMP
CONTEMPORARY ROMANCE

- *Once Upon A Campfire*
- *Second Chance Summer*

ABOUT KAIT

Kait is a Mississippi native, who often swears like a sailor, calls everyone sugar, honey, or darlin', and can wield a bless your heart like a saber or a Snuggie, depending on requirements.

You can find more information on this RITA ® Award-winning author and her books on her website http://kaitnolan.com.

Do you need more small town sass and spark? Sign up for her newsletter to hear about new releases, book deals, and exclusive content!

Lightning Source UK Ltd.
Milton Keynes UK
UKHW022008090223
416682UK00013B/1191